"Do you know what you're doing to me, Lori?"

Hal spoke roughly. "It's all I can do to keep my hands off you. I want you, and I'm sure you want me every bit as much. Maybe, with time, I'll get you out of my system."

Laurel's head reeled. "You talk as if I were some particularly nasty form of infection," she spat at him. "Something that has to be lived through until you develop an immunity! What is it you want from me? Some form of aversion therapy to cure you?"

As she flung the words at him, Laurel realized exactly what she'd said. *I* and *me*. She had been thinking of Lorraine at the start, but somehow something had changed. The savage pain she felt was all her own....

KATE WALKER chose the Brontë sisters, the development of their writing from childhood to maturity, as the topic for her master's thesis. It is little wonder, then, that she should go on to write romance fiction. She lives in the United Kingdom with her husband and son, and when she isn't writing, she tries to keep up with her hobbies of embroidery, knitting, antiques and, of course, reading.

Books by Kate Walker

HARLEQUIN PRESENTS
1053—BROKEN SILENCE

HARLEQUIN ROMANCE
2783—GAME OF HAZARD
2826—ROUGH DIAMOND
2910—CAPTIVE LOVER
2929—MAN OF SHADOWS
2957—THE CINDERELLA TRAP

KATE WALKER

chase the dawn

Harlequin Books

TORONTO • NEW YORK • LONDON
AMSTERDAM • PARIS • SYDNEY • HAMBURG
STOCKHOLM • ATHENS • TOKYO • MILAN

This was always for Mother
In loving memory

Harlequin Presents first edition August 1989
ISBN 0-373-11196-7

Original hardcover edition published in 1988
by Mills & Boon Limited

CHAPTER ONE

'JUST five more minutes,' the dark-haired staff nurse said briskly. 'Then I'm afraid you'll have to go.'

It was strange, Laurel thought to herself, how insistent the nurses were that she shouldn't stay any longer than the time the doctors allowed when nine times out of ten Jenny wasn't even awake for more than a few minutes, and then was usually so hazy with the drugs she had been given that she barely registered her older sister's presence, let alone did anything that might tire her.

Sighing sadly, she considered the slight form in the bed, grimacing in distaste as her glance fell on the tube inserted into her small sister's arm. Even though she had spent so much time here since the accident, just holding Jenny's limp hand, talking all sorts of nonsense in the hope of somehow communicating the fact that she was there and watching endlessly for some slight sign of response, she was still not inured to the sight that had shocked her so much on her first visit.

Jenny's face was so pale it was barely distinguishable from the pillow beneath it; her red hair, several shades brighter than Laurel's own and now cropped short and marred by shaven patches and disfiguring stitches, looked disturbingly gaudy against the whiteness around it. At least the bruises were fading now, the dark purple having changed to a dingy yellow high up on the pale forehead. It seemed impossible that Jenny should have been so battered when Lorraine had been practically unmarked.

Laurel drew in her breath sharply at the thought of her twin. She still could not believe what had happened.

7

In the days since the policewoman had appeared in the shop her brain had been too numbed with shock to register anything other than the fact that Jenny, just six years old, was fighting for her life in a hospital bed.

Oh, *why* had Lorraine come back? It had taken only twenty-four hours for Laurel's life to be turned upside down, her peaceful existence shattered by the sudden return of her twin sister after almost five years' absence. Before she had had time to adjust, the police had sought her out at the flower shop where she worked. They had been very gentle, very sympathetic, but all the sympathy in the world could not alter the fact that Jenny was in a coma in intensive care and Lorraine, whose speeding had caused the accident, had died instantly when her car had collided with an articulated lorry.

A small murmur from the child in the bed brought Laurel's attention swiftly back to her sister.

'Hello, sweetheart,' she said softly, taking the little girl's hand in hers. 'How's my best girl tonight?'

'My legs are sore.' Jenny's voice was little more than a whisper. 'Lauri—it hurts!'

'I know, love,' soothed Laurel, her green eyes clouded with anxiety. 'But the nurse will give you something to make it better when she comes to settle you for the night.'

Jenny was due for another injection soon, she knew. After ten days' almost constant vigil at her sister's bedside she was so well acquainted with the hospital routine that she could almost nurse Jenny herself—as she would probably have to do if she didn't find an answer to her problem very soon. Suddenly a thought seemed to strike the little girl, and with an obvious effort her eyes opened wide.

'Did you bring them?'

'Of course I did—I promised, didn't I?'

'Show me,' Jenny insisted.

Laurel bent her head as she opened the carrier bag at her side, grateful for the fall of her long, red-gold hair that hid the tears that burned in her eyes. Of all the things that Jenny might have wanted to keep with her in the hospital, nothing else could have brought home quite so forcefully the extent of her sister's personal tragedy, and it was all she could do to keep her hand from shaking as she held out the white tap-dancing shoes. Shiny, new, and completely unworn, they had been Laurel's present to Jenny on her sixth birthday just days before the accident. The little girl had started dancing classes six months earlier, and from the first lesson she had been completely hooked. She had a natural ability that her teacher had been quick to recognise, and the shoes had been something she had longed for with all her heart. She was to have worn them in the annual concert when she would have played the part of the Dormouse in *Alice in Wonderland*, but now someone else would wear the quaint, furry costume and it was unlikely that Jenny would ever dance again—not that she knew that yet; she had not been told the full extent of her injuries.

Jenny stirred restlessly, a faint moan escaping her lips.

'It hurts, Lauri. When will it stop hurting?'

'Soon, darling,' Laurel assured her, praying she sounded more confident than she felt.

'In time for the concert?'

Laurel swallowed hard. 'I'm afraid not, poppet. But there'll be other concerts, we'll have you right for them.'

A tear slid weakly down Jenny's cheek, but she did not protest. She groped for Laurel's hand and held it tightly.

'Promise?'

'I promise,' Laurel said firmly, closing her mind against the thought that this was one promise she had very little hope of being able to keep.

A sound at the door announced the arrival of the nurse to settle Jenny for the night. Laurel kissed her sister, assuring her that she would be back early the next day, and left reluctantly. For years she had been the only one to care for Jenny, and it seemed wrong to leave the job to anyone else.

'Off home?' the staff nurse asked brightly as Laurel reached the desk. 'We'll see you tomorrow, then. She seems a bit better today,' she added. 'She's been awake quite a while.'

Laurel nodded silently, wondering to herself which was worse, the still, silent Jenny who had been unconscious for so long, or Jenny awake and in pain.

Barbara was waiting for her outside the ward; steady, reliable Barbara who had proved herself much more than just a friend in the past difficult days.

'How is she?' she asked as they walked down the long, echoing corridor.

'Much the same.' Laurel's tone was dull. 'Still fretting about the concert.'

'That's Jenny. She doesn't know yet?'

Laurel shook her head. 'I can't tell her. She still thinks she's just broken a leg.'

How could she tell her sister that the problem was nothing as simple as a broken bone? Jenny's legs had been almost crushed, her spine badly damaged, and there was only a faint hope that she would ever walk again.

'What about this wonder man—the American surgeon?'

'Oh, he'll operate—if I can get Jenny to him.'

A sense of hopelessness swept over Laurel as she faced up to the full extent of her dilemma. The injury to Jenny's spine would need complicated surgery, and there was one man who had the necessary skill to ensure that she would be able to walk and, more particularly, to dance again. A miracle worker, the hospital surgeon had called him—but he lived and worked in America. If there was anyone who could ensure that Jenny would be able to fulfil her dreams and become once again a healthy, active child instead of the pathetic, white bundle of pain

Laurel now saw every day, then he was the one—but only if Laurel could raise the enormous and, to her, impossible sum needed to cover the flight to America and a lengthy stay in a hospital there.

'No luck at the bank?' Barbara questioned with an anxious glance at her friend's pale face.

Laurel shook her head, sending her mane of copper-coloured hair flying.

'I've nothing to offer as security. The flat's only rented and I've no savings at all. If only Dad had made that fortune he was always talking about—or at least taken out life insurance!'

Barbara Howard reached out and squeezed Laurel's arm sympathetically. She knew how Terry Grahame had drifted from one money-making scheme to another, always believing that *this* was the one that would make his fortune. His latest venture had just collapsed in ruins, leaving him bankrupt once again, when a drunken driver had ploughed his car into a group of people waiting for a bus, killing Laurel's father and his wife. There had been no insurance, the house had already been sold to pay off his debts, and Barbara knew just how hard her friend had found it to make ends meet with an empty bank balance and a baby sister, then only sixteen months old, to support. It was then that Laurel had come to the shop Barbara had just opened, looking for a job.

'If you ask me,' she said bluntly when they were in her car, heading towards Laurel's small flat, 'you're wasting your time trying to raise the money round here. You're missing the obvious answer.'

'What answer? What do you mean, Babs?'

'The missing husband,' Barbara replied crisply. 'What's his name—Rochester? If I remember rightly, Lorraine said he was made of money. That's right, isn't it?'

Laurel nodded slowly, her mind going back to the day when the shop door had opened and she had looked up to find her sister standing in front of her. She had barely had time to take in the expensive clothes, immaculately styled hair and careful make-up before Lorraine had launched into a stream of complaint.

'You can't imagine the trouble I've had to find you! I went to the old flat first, then the neighbours told me you'd moved. The old woman at your new place said you worked in a flower shop but didn't know which one. I've trailed round every shop in town looking for you.'

Laurel's stunned brain noted the high, almost hysterical note in her sister's voice. Something was wrong, this was no casual visit—if any visit after nearly five years' absence could be described as casual.

'Well, the prodigal's back,' Lorraine went on. 'Where's the fatted calf? I'm dying for a really good talk. When do you finish here?'

'Half-five,' Laurel said slowly, still trying to adjust. 'But I have to collect Jenny in ten minutes. She stays with me here for the last couple of hours.'

'Oh yes, Jenny.' Lorraine's smile stiffened. 'How is she?'

'She's fine. She——' Laurel's voice died away as a movement of her twin's hands drew her attention to the thick gold band that gleamed on her wedding finger. 'You're married!' she exclaimed in shock.

''Fraid so!' Lorraine laughed, lifting her hand to wave it under Laurel's nose. Then, suddenly, she let it drop to the counter again, the smile fading from her face. 'Don't look so disapproving. You're not sulking because I didn't invite you, are you?'

Laurel couldn't answer, she was trying to deal with the hurt it caused her to know that her twin had taken such an important step without even letting her know. But then Lorraine had never felt the family loyalty that was so much a part of Laurel's character; she had always put herself first and everyone else came a good way second.

'There wasn't time, anyway,' Lorraine went on defensively. 'And not for the reason you might think, Miss Prim! It's just that Hal's the sort of man who knows what he wants and when he finds it he acts—fast!'

'And he wanted you?' The conviction that something was wrong was growing stronger. Lorraine's casual tone might deceive someone who knew her less well but, even after five years' separation, it did not convince her sister. 'Hal *is* your husband, I take it?'

'Yes.' Lorraine did not meet her sister's eyes. 'Hal Rochester,' she added, almost reluctantly. Then, changing the subject with a swiftness that Laurel found intensely disturbing, she went on, 'If you've got to collect Jenny I'll give you a lift, if you like.'

Outside the shop, Laurel stared in amazement at the sleek white sports car beside which her sister halted.

'This is yours?' she said in disbelief, and Lorraine nodded smugly.

'I told you I'd come back when I was rich!' she declared, and only a sister's ears would have caught the note of bravado in her voice.

'Mr Rochester must be very wealthy,' commented Laurel, watching her twin closely.

'Oh, he is,' Lorraine agreed airily. 'He's absolutely loaded.'

'Well?' Barbara's voice broke in on Laurel's memories. 'Couldn't he afford to pay for Jenny's operation?'

'I think so.' Laurel's green eyes lit with hope for the first time in days, then abruptly clouded again. 'But it's not as easy as that, Babs. They were separated; the marriage had broken down.'

Once more her memories absorbed her. She had only had one night to talk to her sister, but in that time, in response to Laurel's careful questioning, Lorraine had admitted that her marriage had been a mistake from the start, that once he had had a ring on her finger, Hal had neglected her, absorbed himself in his work without

thought or concern for his bride. Indifferent to her loneliness, he had hardly spoken to her. Most days she had
only seen him when he came to bed, sometimes not even
then because she had been asleep by the time he finally
joined her. In the end she had felt she had no alternative
but to leave.

'But surely if you'd talked to him!' Laurel protested.
'Couldn't you have told him how unhappy he was
making you? After all, he must have loved you——'

'Love!' Lorraine broke in, her voice harsh. 'Love had
nothing to do with it. Hal wanted that marriage very
much.' She emphasised the words cynically. 'And I was
fool enough to think that was enough. I was very soon
disillusioned. I married the wrong man, Lauri. Hal
seemed to have everything I was looking for and he didn't
have a wife—so...'

Her voice trailed off and she made a small choking
sound in her throat. The next moment she was sobbing
uncontrollably, the elegant, sophisticated woman dis-
appearing, to be replaced by a desperately unhappy
young girl as tears coursed down her cheeks. Moving
swiftly to her side, Laurel gathered her up in her arms,
holding her close, a hot wave of anger directed at the
unknown Hal Rochester filling her mind. She had never
seen her twin weep like this, not even in the desolate
days after their parents' deaths. When Lorraine spoke
again her voice was inaudible, muffled by the way her
head was pressed against Laurel's shoulder, but she
caught her sister's final words and they added fuel to
the fires of anger in her mind.

'I *loved* him, Lauri, I really loved him—but he just
used me! He didn't care how I felt, all he thought about
was money—money—*money*!' Lorraine's voice rose
hysterically. 'He *cares* about money—it's all he cares
about!'

'Oh, I know Lorraine said he was a hard-hearted
bastard,' Barbara's voice intruded on her thoughts. 'But

from what you've told me, she was no angel herself—and Jenny's not Lorraine, she's a child, for God's sake! Surely he'll feel differently about her? What does this Rochester fellow do, anyway?'

'I don't know,' Laurel admitted. 'I suppose he's a businessman of some sort—Lorraine never said.'

'Well, offer him a business proposition. You don't have to ask for a gift, just a loan at very low interest because you're family. And it's about time you let him know what's happened—you can't keep him in the dark about something like that.'

'No, I can't,' Laurel murmured. She was shocked to realise that she hadn't even thought of this aspect of things before, her anxiety over Jenny having driven everything else from her mind. Even the ordeal of identifying Lorraine's body, the inquest and, finally, the funeral had scarcely touched her, coming at a time when Jenny's life hung in the balance. Even when she had been moved from intensive care, the worry that she might never walk again and the desperate need to find a way of financing the vital operation had left her no time to mourn her dead sister. But then, in a way, Lorraine had been something of a stranger, for Laurel had not seen or heard from her since the day her twin had disappeared so soon after their parents' deaths.

Now, however, the fact of Hal Rochester's existence seemed like a gift from heaven. Barbara was right, she had been dreadfully remiss in not trying to contact him sooner. She would have to find him, tell him about Lorraine, and then maybe, just maybe, he would help. She had his telephone number, she remembered, hope growing in her at the thought that all possibilities hadn't been exhausted. She had seen the brief entry, 'Hal', scrawled at the end of the address section in Lorraine's diary when the police had returned her sister's handbag to her.

In Jenny's bedroom Barbara surveyed the two leather suitcases lying open on the bed.

'What a mess! Was Lorraine always this untidy?'

Laurel shook her head silently, unable to put into words how she had felt when she had seen the clothes, shoes and cosmetics all bundled together without any care even though they were all clearly very expensive items. Such carelessness was so unlike Lorraine, who had always been so concerned with her appearance, that she could only assume that her sister had packed in great haste and in a very disturbed state of mind. She had made no attempt to tidy things; the thought that Lorraine would never wear these clothes again had been too much to bear, and now tears blurred her eyes as Barbara pulled a sheet of paper from the tangled mess in one case.

'Who are the Kenningtons?'

'Who?' asked Laurel, puzzled.

Barbara held the letter towards her so that she could see it came from a London hotel, confirming a booking made for a Mr and Mrs Kennington dating from the weekend before Lorraine's unexpected arrival.

'I don't know the name. Perhaps Lorraine was visiting some friends in London and decided on impulse to come here too.' Discarding the letter, she turned her attention back to to the cases. 'Look, here's a photograph.'

Barbara studied it over her shoulder. 'So that's the opposition,' she commented. 'Doesn't look too terrible, does he?'

Laurel studied the face of the man in the photograph. It was a good-looking face, young, almost boyish, under a thatch of thick fair hair. Bright blue eyes looked directly at the camera with a confident, even cocky expression, as if the man was well aware of his own attractiveness. He certainly looked as if he had plenty of money, to judge by the quality of his suit and shirt— but was he the sort of man who would use that money to help Jenny?

Laurel frowned, noting once more that confident smile, the arrogance in the man's stance, the slight thickening under the jawline that spoke of a degree of self-indulgence that would show more clearly in time. He was Lorraine's type all right, she thought, pain twisting inside her at the thought of the way her twin had drawn boyfriends to her like bees to a honeypot. But from the way Lorraine had talked she had expected someone older, stronger somehow; this man looked much more easy-going than the husband her twin had described. Well, he was Jenny's only hope, and for Jenny's sake she had to find him. Dropping the photograph back on the bed, she reached for Lorraine's handbag and pulled out the diary.

Her hand shook noticeably as she dialled Hal Rochester's number and without realising it she crossed her fingers superstitiously as she waited for someone to answer.

'This is Nunham . . .'

The words blurred as, with a sinking heart, Laurel recognised the impersonal tones of a telephone answering machine. What she had to say could not be communicated on a recorded message. How could she tell a man his wife was dead, however estranged they had been, through the medium of a machine? In a daze, Laurel became aware of the silence at the other end of the line and imagined the tape on the machine turning slowly, recording nothing, then, a fierce wave of embarrassment sweeping over her, she banged down the receiver, shaking her head at her own foolishness.

She had to meet Hal Rochester face to face. She couldn't tell him of Lorraine's death and ask his help for Jenny any other way. A few minutes spent with an atlas told her that Nunham was a small town on the North Yorkshire coast, so small that it seemed finding Hal Rochester should be easy. If not, she had his phone number as a means of contacting him. Once again she lifted the telephone receiver, this time to check on the times of trains to Nunham the next day.

Laurel stood staring out at the wide expanse of the bay that curved round at both ends into high, dangerous cliffs. Behind her, narrow houses clustered round the tiny harbour where the fishermen were busy with their nets, waiting for the tide to turn before they could set sail. Nunham seemed an unlikely place in which to find a man as wealthy as Hal Rochester.

A heavy sigh escaped her as she thought how much Jenny would have loved this place. She had never experienced a proper seaside holiday; Laurel's wages didn't stretch to anything more than a rare day out. In fact she had only had one family holiday herself. A white-hot flash of pain seared through her as she remembered Lorraine as she had been then, alive and laughing, revelling in the rare release from the restrictions her father's improvidence had imposed on their life. Lorraine had always hated being poor, she had detested the shabbiness of their home and resented the fact that she couldn't have new clothes like her friends. Remembering the white sports car, Laurel acknowledged that in the end her sister had found the riches she had always hoped for, but they hadn't brought her happiness, and now—she bit her lip hard, choking back a cry of distress—now it was too late, she would never get a second chance. And somewhere in this town was the man who was responsible for Lorraine's unhappiness.

A mixture of anger and determination drove away Laurel's sorrow. If Hal Rochester had treated Lorraine better she would never have left him, never have come back to Ashingby in such a state of tension that her attention was not fully on her driving when she had taken Jenny to school on that fateful day. In a way he was as responsible for the accident as Lorraine herself. His money could never make up for the way he had treated

Lorraine or bring her back, but it could help Jenny, and right now Jenny was the one with most to lose. She must find Lorraine's husband as soon as possible. Perhaps someone in the small hotel in which she had booked a room would know of him.

'Hello, Mrs Grahame.' Alec Tracey, the landlord of the hotel, greeted Laurel cheerily as she stepped uncertainly into the crowded bar. 'What'll it be, then?'

For a second Laurel was nonplussed, not realising that his words were directed at her, but then, glancing down at her hands and seeing the unaccustomed gleam of gold on the third finger of the left one, she remembered.

At the start of her journey Lorraine's wedding ring had been in her handbag, together with her sister's purse containing her cheque and credit cards and a surprisingly large amount of money which Laurel planned to return to her twin's husband. But during the long train journey she had suffered the persistent attentions of a young soldier travelling home on leave who seemed to feel that, as a single woman travelling alone, she was fair game. Wanting only to be left alone to try and think out just what she was going to say to Hal Rochester when she finally met him, Laurel had been driven to take the ring from the purse with the hasty and, even to her own ears, lame-sounding excuse of having put it there earlier when she had washed her hands and slipped it on her finger. The clumsy strategy had worked: after a few minutes' embarrassed silence the young man had left his seat, muttering something about getting a drink, and did not return. Laurel had forgotten that the ring was still on her finger until the landlord had drawn her attention to it, and of course her signature in the hotel register— L. Grahame—gave no indication of the fact that she was not actually married.

'Oh, just an orange juice, please.'

As she spoke a slight movement drew her attention to the other side of the bar and, turning her head, she found herself staring straight into a pair of eyes that were exactly the blue-green colour of the sea in the bay—and just as cold. The rest of the room seemed to blur, the noise of careless chatter faded as she stood transfixed by the cool insolent gaze levelled at her. She was hazily aware of a tall, masculine form, a mane of dark hair, and an irrational shiver of apprehension slid down her spine as she saw the faint lift of the dark eyebrows before they drew together in a hostile frown as the man's assessing gaze swept over her.

'Your drink, Mrs Grahame.' Alec Tracey's words jolted her back to reality, and with a murmured word of thanks she handed over the correct money, took her glass and glanced round, looking for somewhere to sit, carefully avoiding looking in the direction of the man at the bar.

She found a seat on the opposite side of the room and sat down thankfully, her legs suddenly not quite steady beneath her. That frown, with its undisguised hostility, had shaken her. She could see no reason for it. A large mirror hung on the far wall and, glancing at it surreptitiously, Laurel could see the man reflected in it.

He was a tough-looking character, big, strongly built, with broad shoulders and chest and long legs encased in denim jeans so disreputable that she wondered to herself at the fact that he had ever been allowed into the place. But then, whoever he was, he was evidently well known locally—several times he had broken off his conversation to return the greetings of new arrivals. At first glance she had taken him to be one of the fishermen she had seen earlier, the worn jeans and equally faded denim jacket worn over a navy T-shirt seemed to confirm that impression, but on closer inspection she decided that was not the case.

The thick mane of glossy dark brown hair had once been styled by an expert, though it was now worn rather long, falling over his collar at the back, and the boots he wore were beautifully made, possibly even hand-crafted. But, finally, it was his hands that gave him away. Watching closely as he lifted his glass or acknowledged a greeting, Laurel noted that the long fingers, darkly tanned as they were, bore none of the calluses and broken nails that had marred the hands of the men she had seen repairing their nets. They were strong, square-tipped, and immaculate, not the hands of someone who spent their days hauling nets and gutting fish.

At that moment the man looked up, meeting her eyes in the mirror, blue locking with green for a moment before he raised his glass in a deliberate mockery of a toast. Blushing fierily, Laurel turned away sharply, affecting an interest in a painting over the fireplace, but not before she had seen the narrowing of his eyes in a shrewd, assessing stare mixed with—with what? Anger? Perplexity?

The thought that she might have piqued this insolent stranger by her obvious indifference to his interest pleased Laurel. Of all the people who had stopped to greet him, quite a few had been women, all of them clearly vying for his attention, and he evidently thought so well of himself that he expected that any woman—every woman—would be flattered by his interest in her.

Well, not this woman! Laurel told him silently inside her head, but even as she did so she was forced to wonder just what it was about this man that had put her so much on edge. It wasn't as if she was unused to masculine attention. Without vanity, she knew that her red-gold hair, heart-shaped face with wide green eyes set above high cheekbones and small, full mouth, together with a slenderness that gave an impression of fragile delicacy, was a combination that attracted many men, and she had never had any shortage of possible boyfriends—but this man was different. There was something about the way he had looked at her that frightened her. This was not just the ordinary sexual attraction of a man to a presentable girl; there was something deep in the sea-blue eyes that threatened, some emotion she could not interpret.

The sound of movement behind her drew her attention and a sidelong glance in his direction showed her that the man was preparing to leave. An irrational relief swept through her and she relaxed against the back of her seat. She had only to stay where she was, giving him time to get well away, and then she could go too, making her way to the small bedroom that suddenly seemed like a haven of peace.

As the man moved towards the door a dark shape rose from the floor and followed him without a word of command being spoken. Watching the beautiful black labrador that stayed close to his heels, Laurel had to admit that, whatever her feelings about its owner, the dog was perfectly trained. With a faint sigh she remembered her own childhood longing to own a dog. There had never been enough money to spare to pay for its food, and the constant moves, the increasingly smaller houses and, finally, flats in which they had lived had made it impossible to consider even the smallest puppy.

With the stranger's departure a great feeling of tiredness swept through Laurel. It was as if the irritation he had caused her had been all that was keeping her exhaustion at bay, and she thought longingly of the comfortable-looking bed upstairs. But first she needed some fresh air. Her head felt stuffy and thick after the time she had spent in the smoke-filled bar.

A light sea mist had descended with the evening, and it swirled damply round her as she crossed the pebbled courtyard to the narrow street, slowly breathing in the salt-tanged air, feeling the tension in her neck and shoulders gradually slacken. She had been foolish to let the man disturb her so much. Really, she should have been flattered that such an attractive man should take an interest in her—and he *was* attractive, she admitted unwillingly, very attractive in a tough, dangerous sort of way. In this town, in another century, he could have been a smuggler, a pirate even—with those rakish good looks all he needed was a gold ear-ring to complete the picture.

'Lauri——' A low, husky voice behind her broke in on her fanciful thoughts.

It took Laurel just seconds to spin round, responding automatically to the use of her name, but those seconds were long enough for her to realise that she had made a mistake. No one in Nunham could even know her name, let alone use it with such obvious familiarity. But the realisation came too late. She had already turned and found herself only feet away from the dark, insolent stranger who had come up behind her silently out of the mist.

He was standing watching her, long hands resting lightly on his hips, his tall frame dwarfing Laurel's own five feet six inches, powerful and menacing, the blue eyes alert and watchful so that he saw her instinctive glance around the street, searching for someone to whom she could call for help. There was no one; the narrow street was deserted. Laurel's throat dried in fear. She was alone and frighteningly vulnerable.

'What do you want?'

She had meant the words to sound defiant, but they came out in a hoarse, barely audible croak. But he heard them and a slow, sardonic smile spread across his previously expressionless face.

'What sort of a question is that?' he drawled smoothly. 'I want *you* of course. I've been looking for you everywhere.'

Laurel found she was having trouble breathing, her heart was thudding painfully as she stood paralysed, a vivid image of all the rape cases she had ever heard of or read about filling her mind. What sort of man was this?

'And now I've found you——'

The single step he took towards her was enough to break the spell that held Laurel frozen and, swinging away from him, she began to run desperately, her footsteps echoing loudly in the deserted street. She heard no sound behind her but was suddenly dimly aware of a dark shape flashing past her, and she slid to a halt as the black labrador appeared in front of her, effectively blocking her way, a low growl warning her not to try to pass him.

She turned in panic to see the man approaching unhurriedly, the hateful smile that curved his lips revealing that her attempt at escape had done little more than amuse him. Who *was* he? How did he know her name? Slowly she backed away, her breath escaping in a small, choking cry as she came hard up against a wall. Her eyes wide pools of fear in a very white face, she turned to her pursuer.

'Who are you?' she demanded in a trembling voice. 'What do you want?'

'Come off it, Lauri!' He sounded irritated now, the silky mockery gone from his voice. 'You know damn well who I am.'

'I don't!' Laurel's protest was high and sharp. 'I don't know you from Adam! I've never seen you before in my life!'

The frown that darkened his features terrified her and he halted abruptly, regarding her with cynical disbelief.

'Now look, Lauri,' he said, and his voice was low, dangerous. 'I don't know what game you're playing, but it isn't going to work. You know exactly who I am and I, for my sins, am well aware of just who you are. Even though our marriage was such a very brief affair, I could never forget my beloved wife.'

CHAPTER TWO

LAUREL'S brain reeled sickeningly. This couldn't be happening! 'My beloved wife,' he had said with a bitterness that spoke volumes for the feelings behind the words—and he had used her name—or, rather, Lorraine's—for she realised now that it must have been *Lori* he had said, and she had taken it for her own name.

It came as no surprise that he had taken her for Lorraine—she and her twin had always been so alike that even their parents had had difficulty telling them apart—but could this man really be Lorraine's husband, this arrogant, bullying monster who spoke so scathingly of his wife? If he was, then it was no wonder Lorraine had left him, no wonder she had seemed so distraught. But he looked nothing like the man in the photograph. He was older too, somewhere around thirty, Laurel guessed. He was watching her closely, waiting for some response, the intensity of his gaze so disturbing that she had to swallow hard before she could speak.

'I'm not your wife.' She tried hard to make her tone calmly reasonable but didn't quite succeed, that high-pitched note of fear still lingered. 'You've made a mistake! I——'

'OK, lady, you get your Oscar.' The coolly cynical tone cut off her attempt to explain. 'You put on a very fine performance and no doubt it would convince someone who didn't know the truth, but it does nothing for me. You're my wife, that's my ring you're wearing. I haven't forgotten the day I put it on your finger even if you have. And I saw your name in the hotel register—Lorraine——'

'No!' Laurel tried to protest, but he let her get no further.

'No,' he agreed silkily, 'not Lorraine *Grahame*, is it, my lovely? It's Lorraine Rochester, as I know to my cost. And don't try inventing some story of a long-lost sister. You told me yourself that you've no family, so don't try and make up one now.'

Laurel's eyes widened in shock. Lorraine had told him that she was alone in the world! The stab of pain at her twin's denial of her own existence took her breath away, but a moment later it was driven away by the realisation of the way that fact made her situation so very much more difficult, knowing that the mind of this dark, tormenting man was already closed against the only explanation she could give him. With bitter irony she saw that the truth was the one thing he would not believe.

'Nothing to say?' the man taunted, his sea-coloured eyes as cold as his voice. 'That's not like you, Lori.'

'Please listen,' Laurel began, then hesitated, faltering beneath that steady, icy gaze. An image of Lorraine's face as she had last seen her alive floated before her eyes and she felt the sting of tears as she recalled her sister's desperate unhappiness, unhappiness that was easily explained if her twin had loved *this* man. To her distress she felt a trickle of moisture slide slowly down one cheek.

'Heaven spare me!' The man before her sighed his exasperation. 'Lori, I know all your tricks, there's nothing to be gained by trotting them all out. Look——' He reached for Laurel's left hand, lifting it to the level of her eyes. 'Tell me one thing,' he said, his voice coldly reasonable. 'Is this the ring that Hal Rochester bought for his wife?'

A weak wave of relief swept over Laurel. Here at last was a question her bruised mind could answer without difficulty. The memory of Lorraine still lingered, depriving her of speech, but she nodded numbly.

'Progress at last! Now, as you seem to have been afflicted with a sudden attack of amnesia, perhaps I'd better remind you of who I am.' He made a small, mocking bow over her hand, and she fought against the desire to snatch it away, to lash out at him with all her strength and wipe the taunting mockery from his face. 'My name is Hal Rochester,' he said slowly and clearly as if explaining a difficult lesson to a rather stupid child, 'and you are——'

Laurel's lips were dry and she wetted them nervously with her tongue. There was only one thing she could tell him, and she knew before she spoke that he would not believe it.

'I'm Lauri Grahame,' she croaked hoarsely, unconsciously using the form of her name—or her sister's—that he had used earlier.

Hal Rochester shook his head with an angry movement. 'Not good enough,' he stated adamantly.

'But I'm not——' Laurel forced herself to try again, flinching away from his savage scowl, 'I'm *not* Lorraine—she's——' The word seemed to swell in her throat, choking her, she still couldn't believe that it was true and she had to force it out. 'Lorraine's dead and——'

'Lady, there have been times when I wished you were,' Hal cut in on her violently. 'If you persist with this farce I won't be answerable for the consequences. Do you expect me to doubt the evidence of my own eyes? Who *are* you?' he rapped out, clearly losing his tenuous grip on his temper.

Laurel's tongue seemed to have frozen inside her mouth; she could find no words to answer him. She had told him the truth and, as she had expected, he had not believed her—so what had she to lose by using Lorraine's name? The crazy thought slipped into her mind from nowhere. Everything Hal Rochester had said implied that his wife was the last person he wanted to see. Perhaps if she told him what he wanted to hear then he would go and leave her alone. But what about Jenny if he did?

Her heart twisted at the thought of her little sister so far away, alone and in pain. This man was Jenny's last chance of a healthy future. But would he offer them the help they needed? A surreptitious glance at his hard-boned face, his mouth set in a grim, straight line, made her feel that she could have little hope that he would. He looked as if he didn't know what kindness meant, let alone that he would be prepared to offer it to two complete strangers he didn't believe existed. It was no wonder that Lorraine had fled from this callous, bullying creature!

'Lori——' Hal prompted coldly, and the sound of his voice sent a shiver of fear down Laurel's spine. She had never felt so vulnerable in her life. Her mind seemed to split in two, one half wanting, for the sake of her twin, to round on him, shout that she detested him for the way he had treated Lorraine, the other, with thoughts of Jenny uppermost, trying desperately to think of a way to pacify him, calm him so that he would listen—and the conflict left her totally incapable of saying anything. Through the haze of confusion that filled her head she heard Hal's impatient curse.

'I think we need to talk,' he said curtly. 'But not here. We'll go to your room.'

'No!' Laurel found her voice at last.

'Well, we can't stay here all night. So you'd better make up your mind—your room or my place, it's up to you.'

Laurel shuddered slightly at the choice he offered. Wherever Hal's 'place' might be it would be enemy territory, putting her at an immediate disadvantage.

'My room, then,' she conceded grudgingly.

'A pity,' Hal murmured drily. 'You've never seen Highcliff, you don't know what you're missing.'

He turned towards the hotel, still holding her wrist imprisoned in his strong grip, and mutinously Laurel tried to shake off his encircling grasp, only to have it tighten even further until she felt it might crush the delicate bones.

'I won't run away!' she protested sharply, a sense of despair filling her at the thought that there was nowhere she could run to; he would only follow her wherever she went.

'You did once before,' said Hal in a quiet voice that nevertheless held a note of warning that crushed her impotent rebellion before it had had time to form. 'I don't intend to let that happen again, not till we've talked things out.'

Once inside the hotel, Laurel was relieved to find the reception desk empty so that she could collect her key without anyone seeing her. She had dreaded the prospect of anyone meeting her while she was with Hal, let alone seeing her take him up to her room. As she turned to the stairs she glanced uncertainly at the labrador, still close at Hal's heel. Hal saw the doubt on her face and his lips curled in a mocking smile.

'He'll wait here if I tell him, but Jet's well known around here, everyone knows who he belongs to. If he's seen, people might put two and two together and come up with some interesting answers.'

'He'd better come with us, then,' Laurel responded stiffly. The fewer people who knew of her association with Hal, the better.

At her door she hesitated, the key in her hand, unable to take the step of unlocking it and letting this hateful man into her room. A half-formed plan of dashing inside and slamming the door in his face rose in her mind, only to subside swiftly when Hal, clearly anticipating some such reaction, took the key from her hand and inserted it into the lock himself, pushing the door open with one hand before bundling her unceremoniously into the room and slamming the door shut behind them.

Panic almost choked her as she saw how he calmly pocketed the key and then, with a word of command to the dog who obediently lay down beside the door, strolled around the room, his eyes narrowing thoughtfully as he took in the few personal belongings she had left out. Laurel eyed him warily like a small, trapped animal watching some sleekly dangerous predator. When she had unpacked earlier the room had seemed small but adequate, now she felt irrationally that it had somehow shrunk to tiny proportions, scarcely seeming large enough to contain the height and breadth of this man as he flung open the wardrobe and considered her small collection of clothes, which looked rather lost and pathetic in the large interior.

'You obviously weren't planning on a long stay,' he commented drily, reaching out to flick through the clothes with swift, disdainful movements. An odd intonation in his voice made Laurel glance at him curiously, but his back was still towards her and she could see nothing of his face.

With the full force of those mesmeric eyes turned away from her she was able to think a little more rationally. What would happen if, now that he was calmer, less aggressive, she tried once more to tell him the truth? Her own identity would be easy enough to prove; she had her cheque book and card in her bag, he would have to believe that. But what would happen then? Would he feel any sympathy for the family of the wife he so obviously despised? Oh, Lorraine, she thought on a stab of pain, how did you ever get involved with this man? What sort of life had her twin led before she had run away from Hal Rochester? Laurel started violently as Hal swung round suddenly.

'Why did you come here, Lori?' he demanded, his blue eyes dark with cold anger, seeming to bore into her as if they could reach right to her soul. 'Just what do you want this time? Is it a divorce you're after, or is it money again? Is that it, Lori? Is it money you want?'

Laurel's heart sank before the fury that darkened his face, her hopes of helping Jenny crumbling into ashes before they were even fully formed. If Hal hated his wife so much, he would never consider helping her family— a family he didn't even believe existed.

'I don't want anything from you!' she declared bravely, forcing her eyes to meet his. But she had hesitated just a second too long, and Hal nodded grimly.

'Oh yes, you do, my lovely wife. It's written all over your pretty face. Your bank account's empty again, so you've come running back to me for another hand-out. What the hell you do with it all I can't imagine. OK, lady, how much is it going to cost me this time?'

'I've told you I don't want your money!' Laurel flung the words at him. Hal's contemptuous words, his scathing tone, sickened her. In the back of her mind she could hear Lorraine's heartbroken voice saying, 'All he thought about was money,' and her palms itched to slap his face, wipe that condescending sneer from it. How dared he accuse her twin of anything after the way he had treated her!

'Oh, I know what you've told me,' Hal dismissed her vehement protest with a shrug. 'But I know your infinite capacity for lying—though I must admit that this is a new routine. I thought I knew every trick of yours, but this outraged innocence is quite something else. You'd make things a lot easier if you just came straight out with it. How much do you want? A couple of thousand? More?'

Laurel stared at him aghast. Lorraine had told her that Hal Rochester was wealthy, but, as she saw him so scruffily dressed, the thought had crossed her mind that perhaps he no longer had quite so much money. Now he was offering her thousands of pounds as easily as she might have offered Jenny a pound or two—more easily, she admitted ruefully, remembering just how hard she had found it to make ends meet. It seemed so cruel that she could not even ask him for a loan when he could so obviously afford it.

Hal was still clearly convinced that she was Lorraine, he had expected her to ask for money, and it seemed he was actually prepared to give her just as much as she wanted. But she wasn't her twin and, despite the fact that her—or rather, Jenny's—need was far greater than Lorraine's might ever have been, he wouldn't give her a penny—mainly because he didn't believe she existed. And even if she proved that she did exist, by showing him her cheque book or some other evidence, wasn't he likely to just walk out, leave her without a second thought when he knew she wasn't the wife he at least felt some financial responsibility for?

Recalling how she had been tempted to pretend to be Lorraine in the hope that Hal would leave her alone, Laurel admitted to herself that it would be frighteningly easy to claim to be Lorraine now and take the money he offered. It was clear that the amount would mean little to him, but it would mean everything to Jenny. *No*, she couldn't do it. In all the years she had cared for Jenny she had prided herself on the fact that every penny she had spent had been come by honestly. That was why she had taken the job in Barbara's shop, abandoning her own modest ambitions of going to teacher-training college in order to make sure that her young sister was properly cared for. It was a bitter irony that Lorraine, who had done nothing to help with Jenny in the past, would now have been able to provide everything her little sister needed, but—Laurel caught back a choking cry of anguish—Lorraine was dead and Jenny faced a lifetime of pain, unable to walk, if Laurel didn't do something to help her.

'How much?' Hal demanded savagely, taking a step towards her, and in a reaction of sheer, unthinking panic, Laurel blurted out the amount the hospital doctor had told her Jenny's surgery would cost.

For a moment even Hal looked taken aback, the frown that darkened his face sending a shiver down Laurel's spine.

'So much?' he said slowly. 'You're really in deep this time, aren't you, my lovely?'

'It's not for——' Laurel tried one last-ditch attempt to explain, but Hal wasn't listening.

'Well, I said you could have it and I'll keep to that—but on certain conditions.'

'Conditions?' The word escaped before she had time to think if it was wise. Hal was offering her every penny of the money she needed for Jenny's operation—no, not her, he was offering it to *Lorraine*—but he wanted something in return. What if those conditions were something she, Laurel, could fulfill? Wouldn't that put this transaction on the terms of the business deal Barbara had talked about? 'What sort of conditions?'

'Oh, don't worry,' Hal derided. 'They'll be no more difficult than they were before. But first you'll have to drop this pretence that you're not Lorraine.'

'But I'm not——' The need to have him know the truth gave Laurel no time to wonder what that 'no more difficult than they were before' had meant.

'Damn you, Lori!' Hal exploded so violently that Laurel shrank away from him in fear. 'I've had all I can take of this! Either you're Lorraine and you've got a chance of getting what you want or you're not—in which case you leave empty-handed, because I swear to you that only my wife will get anything from me. Is that clear?'

Laurel could only nod numbly. The burning intensity of Hal's eyes, the fierce conviction in his voice, told her only too clearly that he meant every word he said.

'You're my wife, Lori,' Hal went on, the cold, precise statement stinging Laurel's raw nerves like the lash of sleety rain. 'And as my wife you've been kept in the manner to which you were only too pleased to become accustomed—and for that you owe me. All I'm asking is that you come back and live with me again.'

'Never!' Laurel's response was automatic. She couldn't stand another moment in this man's company, let alone live with him. 'I won't do it!'

'Fine.' Hal's offhand remark was the last thing she had expected. 'In that case I'll say goodbye.'

Her mind too dazed to think, Laurel watched him walk towards the door. Only moments before his departure had been all that she had wanted, but that was when she had been thinking only of herself. Now all that she knew was that if she let him go he took Jenny's only chance of a future with him. Her lips parted to call him back, but the words froze on her tongue. He had said that he would only give the money to his wife, to Lorraine. The only way she could hope to help Jenny now was by pretending to be her twin. Her mind shrank away from the thought of such deceit.

Oh, Jenny, she thought on a searing flash of anguish. *I did everything I could*—— The key was in the lock, the door swung open, and in her head she could hear her small sister's voice saying, 'It hurts, Lauri. When will it stop hurting?' and her own foolhardy promise that one day Jenny would dance again.

'Wait——'

The word was barely audible, but Hal caught it and turned, his hand still on the door.

'What—what exactly would I have to do?'

'Just what I said. I want you to come back and live with me again for the next two months.'

'But why?' It didn't seem possible that a man who so obviously hated and despised his wife should suddenly want her to live with him again.

The look Hal turned on her seared her from top to toe like a flash of lightning.

'I don't need to answer that question, do I? Or is that something else you've conveniently forgotten along with who you are? Look, all that I'm asking is that you live in my house, act the part of my wife in public——'

'Nothing else?'

Laurel's voice was weak with tension and a wave of relief swamped her as she saw Hal shake his head. His reasons for wanting a wife back, that enigmatic 'I don't need to answer that question, do I?' didn't matter if a wife in name only was all he wanted. Surely she could manage that? Two months weren't so very long when balanced against the rest of Jenny's life, especially when it seemed that this was the only way she could have any hope of obtaining the money she needed so desperately. And that 'in name only' was the one thing that made this nightmarish bargain possible; it put the matter of the money back on a business footing. Although she knew it was Lorraine Hal was offering the money to, if she fulfilled the terms he demanded then she would have earned it just as much as her twin could have done.

'Come on, Lori,' goaded Hal. 'How long does it take to say yes? You need money, you can have it—on my terms. If you're very good I'll throw in the divorce as well.'

'I don't need a divorce!' Laurel protested in panic. If Hal started any such proceedings he would find out the truth about Lorraine—— Her stomach lurched sickeningly as she realised how, without quite being sure how it had happened and without it being explicitly stated, she had been manoeuvred into a position where Hal believed she had dropped the 'pretence' of being someone else and was in fact admitting that she was Lorraine. She was already entangled in the deceit and lies that involved. 'Just the money will do,' she managed, her struggle to come to terms with her outraged conscience making the words come out in a brittle voice that sounded hard and flippant.

'I thought it might.'

Hal's bitter taunt, the scathing contempt that darkened his eyes, were more than Laurel could take. Anger boiled up inside her, driving away her doubts about her actions on a floodtide of hatred for this man who had treated her twin so badly and who had driven her into this impossible situation. He didn't care why she needed the money—he hadn't even asked. All he wanted was to use her need to force her to do exactly as he pleased, to exert his power over her, just as he had rushed Lorraine into a marriage that had made her desperately unhappy. With a sharp cry she lashed out at him with all her strength, jerking his head to one side as her palm struck his cheek. But the cry changed to a whimper of fear and pain as Hal's hands came up to close viciously around her arms, holding her still when she would have swung away from him. Above the livid red mark of her fingers on his face the sea-coloured eyes were coldly calm.

'So there is some of the old Lori in there after all. I was beginning to wonder if I'd got the right woman, but now I know I have——'

He stopped suddenly, staring down into Laurel's pale face, and she saw him blink hard as if he didn't quite believe what he saw. When he spoke again his voice had a new, strangely husky note in it.

'Do you know, Lori, this pretence of righteous anger suits you, I've never seen you looking so——'

His dark head moved so swiftly that Laurel had no time to anticipate his intention before her mouth was captured in a bruising, punishing kiss that crushed her lips against her teeth. For a moment she struggled impotently against Hal's strength, but her movements only made him tighten his grip even more, rendering her incapable of movement so that there was nothing she could do but submit to his hateful embrace. With an effort she forced herself to stay still and passive in his arms, fighting the need to escape, trying to shut her mind off from what was happening to her body.

But as soon as she stopped struggling something infinitely more disturbing made her mind blur in shock and horror. Feeling her surrender, Hal deliberately changed his kiss from one meant to hurt and punish to a genuinely sensual caress, his mouth softening on hers, his tongue probing her lips in enticing invitation. Immediately Laurel's blood seemed to burn at white heat in her veins, her mouth opened under Hal's and she swayed towards him, her head swimming as she vaguely registered the fact that his hands were sliding down her arms, linking at the base of her spine to draw her closer. She felt that she had completely lost her sanity as she realised without doubt, without hope of redemption, that she would do anything this man wanted, anything at all, if he would only hold her like this and kiss her until she was incapable of rational thought.

His touch seemed to scorch her and yet she never wanted him to let go. She wanted to feel the hard strength of his body against hers, wanted—— She was jolted back to reality with a suddenness that was shockingly painful as Hal's lips left hers and he lifted his head to look down into her wide green eyes.

'There,' he murmured huskily, 'does that help you to make up your mind? Will it be such a dreadful way to earn your money?'

Recoiling in horror, as much from herself and her unexpected reactions as from Hal, Laurel twisted out of his arms and took several unsteady steps backwards, her eyes fixed on that hard, mocking face. She couldn't go through with this! How could she spend two months with this man?

But she *had* to go through with it. She had a sudden, vivid image of Jenny's life—permanently disabled, possibly confined to a wheelchair—if she didn't. Was she going to let Hal Rochester ruin Jenny's life as he had ruined Lorraine's? Once more she felt that burning hatred towards her sister's husband and welcomed it as it obliterated every doubt and fear.

'That wasn't part of our bargain!' she flashed at him. 'In future you'll keep your hands to yourself. If you don't the deal's off!' The sardonic smile that curled Hal's lips almost destroyed her new-found courage, but she forced herself to go on. 'And about the money—I'll need some of it immediately—about half of it.' Things would need setting in motion, she would have to have some money ready to hand for the things Jenny would need. Jenny—she was the most important thing—the *only* thing she could let herself think of.

'You'll get it. I'll write a cheque.'

'In cash!' Laurel broke in sharply, realising belatedly that a cheque made out to Lorraine Rochester would be of no earthly use to her. She saw the way Hal's mouth twisted in distaste at her tone and knew a bitter sense of despair at the realisation that she had no defence against his contempt for her. She was embroiled in this deceit now, there was no way out.

'In cash,' Hal agreed coldly. 'I'll bring it tomorrow when I come to fetch you. The two months start from then—I'm not taking the chance you might still run out on me. I'll be here some time around eleven.'

Laurel nodded numbly. She had hoped for a little time to get used to the idea, but perhaps it would be best to plunge straight in, not giving herself time to think. Once more Hal's mouth curved into a smile, but one that Laurel saw with a shiver did not touch his eyes, they remained as cold and hard as ever.

'Don't look so terrified, my lovely,' he said softly. 'It's not the end of the world—it's only two months.'

Only two months! The words repeated over and over in Laurel's head long after the door had closed behind Hal and she heard his footsteps descending the stairs. *Only two months.* Right now, that sounded like an eternity.

CHAPTER THREE

A SHARP rap at her door announced Hal's arrival well before Laurel was mentally ready the next morning, and without waiting for her to respond he strode into the room, taking in her small case lying on the bed in one swift glance.

'I'm glad to see you're ready, I don't have time to waste hanging around waiting for you.'

That's blatantly obvious! Laurel was tempted to retort. There were still a few minutes to go before eleven o'clock and, with every nerve quiveringly sensitive to the primitive force of his physical presence, she couldn't help wishing that he had delayed his arrival slightly to give her much-needed time to prepare herself. Not that she could ever really hope to be prepared for what was to come, she admitted to herself, the hair on the back of her neck lifting in instinctive response like those of a wary cat as Hal came closer.

He looked only a shade less disreputable this morning, in black jeans and sleeveless T-shirt that clung to his muscular chest, emphasising the width of his shoulders, the strength of arms that were as deeply tanned as his face. He didn't get that tan here, Laurel reflected. So far it had been a typically English summer, the bright sun outside bringing the first really warm weather they had had. Her nose wrinkled as she caught the faint tang of a scent she couldn't place, but then she noticed that the dark hair was still damp and, recollecting exactly where she was, she realised that he must have been swimming before heading for the hotel.

Bitterly she contrasted the enjoyable way Hal had spent the first part of the morning with her own frantic preparations. She had had to ring the doctor responsible for Jenny's treatment to let him know that she would be able to finance the necessary surgery. He had been delighted by the news and promised to contact the American specialist as soon as she rang off.

'Though he won't be able to do anything for a while,' he warned. 'We'll have to be sure she's strong enough to travel first, but I'll put things in motion straight away.'

'I won't be able to get back to Ashingby for a time.' Laurel's voice shook on the last words. With every minute that passed that time seemed to stretch ahead further and further until she felt that she would never get to the end of it. 'But I'll ring the hospital every day.' Surely even Hal Rochester would let her use the phone when she needed to—though what explanation she would give him for her frequent long-distance calls she had no idea.

Laurel put the receiver down with a sense of having burned her boats. There was no going back now, she was committed to playing out the role Hal had decreed for her. The second phone call was rather more difficult—even to Barbara she couldn't admit the truth of what had happened, and so she stumbled through a clumsy explanation, telling her friend that Hal had offered the money she needed in return for her services as his housekeeper for a time.

'But where will you be?' Barbara asked anxiously. 'Where can I contact you in an emergency?'

Laurel's mind flinched away from the prospect. She hated being away from Jenny at such a time, but if, in the end, it meant that the little girl would dance again then all the heartache would be worthwhile.

'I have a phone number——' She hunted in her handbag for Lorraine's diary and read out the number to her friend. 'But Babs, don't ring unless it's absolutely necessary,' she added urgently, imagining with a shudder of horror the possible repercussions if her friend asked to speak to Laurel Grahame. 'I'll contact you—but if you do have to phone, ask for Lauri—that's the name Mr Rochester knows me by. And Babs——' her voice cracked painfully and she had to swallow hard before she could continue, 'give Jenny all my love and tell her I'll ring her every single day.'

Tears filled her eyes as she put the phone down. She hadn't even had time to say goodbye to Jenny properly. The little girl had been drowsy from an injection when she had called at the hospital on her way to the station and she wasn't quite sure how much of her explanation her sister had taken in. But at the time it hadn't mattered quite so much, she had expected to be back in Ashingby in a day or so—now the time before she would see Jenny again stretched ahead endlessly. At least she knew that Barbara would visit every evening. Jenny loved the other woman, looking on her as the aunt she had never had— but it wasn't the same as being there herself.

A sudden movement jolted Laurel out of her unhappy reverie, coming back to the present with a start as Hal tossed a thick brown envelope on to the bed beside her case.

'I'm keeping my half of the bargain,' he stated curtly, and she caught the note of warning in his voice, so clear that he might actually have added, 'Now you keep yours.' 'Not going to count it?' he added tauntingly. 'Aren't you afraid I'll cheat you?'

'I don't think you'd do that,' Laurel responded woodenly, surprising herself by believing what she said. Cruel and callous Hal might be, but there was some-thing about him that told her intuitively he was not a man to go back on his word.

Hal inclined his dark head slightly, his blue eyes coolly assessing. 'So you admit that I play things straight? And what about you?'

'I'll keep my word.' And she would. He'd get full value out of this detestable bargain, it was the only way she could live with what she'd done.

'No second thoughts?'

For the first time Laurel lifted her eyes to his, forcing herself to meet his narrowed gaze. If only he knew! Lying awake in the night, she'd had second, third, and even fourth thoughts about the whole business, debating whether the end justified the means, whether Jenny's need outweighed the distasteful deception she had undertaken. She had tried endlessly to think of some other solution, her own natural inclination to face Hal with the truth warring with the belief that, even if he knew the whole story, he would never consider helping Jenny, particularly not after the way she had let him believe she was Lorraine last night. She held out no hope that he would feel any sympathy for Jenny's plight, he had shown himself to be without any finer feelings of compassion or consideration, and now, looking into the cold, hard mask of his face, she knew that the way she had taken had been the only way.

'None at all.' She hid her distress behind a carefully assumed flippancy and saw his face darken in response.

'You must want this money one hell of a lot,' he said grimly. 'Whatever your reasons, they're important enough to make you forget just how much you hate me. The next two months should be very interesting.'

A moment later his frown had changed to one of distaste as his gaze slid over her slender body in the simple blue cotton dress.

'Where did you get that rag? It does nothing for you.'

'I wear what I like!'

Laurel's chin came up defiantly. She knew the dress was past its best, but it had been pretty when she had bought it and she hadn't been able to afford to replace it.

'You can't like *that*,' Hal derided. Strong hands closed over Laurel's shoulders, swinging her round to face the mirror set in the wardrobe door. 'Take a good look at yourself,' he ordered.

Seeing herself through Hal's critical eyes, Laurel had to admit that she looked shabby, the dress limp and faded after many washes, her pale face showing the effects of the stress of the past couple of weeks, and her hair hanging loose and unstyled over her shoulders, its glowing auburn colour dulled through lack of attention. It was hardly surprising she looked this way, she hadn't had the time or the energy to think about herself lately. Usually she took a great deal of pride in her appearance, although she didn't have the overwhelming interest in clothes and make-up Lorraine had always had.

'What happened to the clothes you took with you?' Hal demanded, and the memory of the expensive, stylish garments bundled together in her twin's suitcases combined with fear of discovery to put a sharp edge on her voice as she declared, 'That's none of your business!'

'While you're with me I'm making it my business. I don't want my wife looking as if she buys her clothes from jumble sales.'

Laurel heard Hal's words with only half her mind, because as she looked into the mirror once more her own image blurred and she saw instead Lorraine as she had looked when she had appeared in the shop on the day she had returned to Ashingby. Even though she was obviously distressed, she had been superbly groomed in an elegant cream suit, not a hair out of place. Lorraine had always loved beautiful clothes and as a teenager she had hated the restrictions imposed by the family's lack of money which had meant that she could have none of the fashionable dresses her friends wore. Laurel bit down hard on her lower lip, forcing back the sob that almost escaped her. Her twin had finally found the luxuries she craved, but they hadn't brought her any happiness.

Hal's possessive 'my wife' sounded in her head, making her shiver in reaction. Her sister hadn't been a person to her husband, just a beautiful possession. He only cared about how she looked because of the way it would reflect on *him*.

Unable to face the image of herself, so like her twin and yet so very different, Laurel made a move to turn away from the mirror, but a perceptible tightening of the hard fingers gripping her shoulders made her suddenly intensely aware of Hal's presence behind her. Her movement brought her up against the hardness of his chest, the warmth of his body reaching her through the thin material of her dress, that tangy mixture of the sea and his own, more personal scent tantalising her nostrils so that she found it difficult to breathe naturally. Her heart was thudding high up in her chest and her palms felt damp. With an effort she stared straight ahead, schooling her face into a stiff mask that revealed nothing of the turmoil inside her.

'What *have* you been doing to yourself, Lori?' asked Hal, a husky, seductive note entering his voice so that, for a moment, Laurel almost deluded herself that he was genuinely concerned. It was so long since she had heard that sort of sympathy in a man's voice, and a sense of weakness assailed her so that she had to fight against an almost irresistible urge to relax and lean back against him, to feel his strength support her. 'You don't look like the same woman,' Hal murmured against her hair, and Laurel's precarious hold on her self-control slipped dangerously. She couldn't go through with this! Twisting out of his grasp, she rounded on him, her hands clenched into small, tight fists at her side.

'That's because I'm not the same woman!' she declared stormily, and would have gone on, told him everything, but the lazy lifting of one dark eyebrow, cynically questioning her statement, froze the words on her lips.

'And just what do you mean by that?' drawled Hal, his indolent tone belied by the alert, watchful expression in his cold blue eyes.

For a long, fraught moment no words would come. *Because I'm not Lorraine, I'm Laurel!* The words burned on her tongue, her conscience urging her to speak them, but her mind warred with her instinctive honesty with a ferocity that threatened to tear her in two. Think of Jenny, an insistent little voice cried inside her head. Think of Jenny and Lorraine, and the way this man treated her. The image of Lorraine's unhappy face still lingered in her mind and a swift glance at those icy blue eyes hardened her resolve.

'Well, look at me!' she snapped, hiding the conflict in her thoughts behind a show of irritation. 'Do you think I like dressing like this?'

'Not your usual style, I'll admit,' Hal murmured ironically. 'But I should have thought the money you took with you was enough to keep anyone—even you— in the manner to which you'd become accustomed. Your ability to go through money always was phenomenal, but this time you've really excelled yourself. What is it, Lori? What sort of a mess are you in?'

Hal's voice had changed on the last two questions. That husky, almost concerned note was back, infinitely destructive to her resolution and composure as doubt tormented her, tearing at her heart. Oh God, had she got it all wrong? Had Lorraine told her the truth? She was well aware of the fact that, as Barbara had said, her twin was no angel. Was it likely that she had been completely innocent in the break-up of her marriage? But Lorraine had been devastated, lost, despairing in a way Laurel had never seen before. Hal Rochester showed no sign of any such feelings. He acted as if he didn't give a damn about his wife, as if all he was concerned about was the money she was costing him. Once more

Lorraine's words came back to haunt her. 'All he thought about was money—money—money!'

Had Hal ever used that money for anything other than his own selfish ends—as he was using it now to force her, as the wife he believed her to be, to stay with him when it was the last thing she wanted? Privately, she doubted it. Well, *she* would do it, in spite of him and without his knowledge, she would use that money in a far more humanitarian way than he—or even Lorraine—had ever done.

'That's my own business!' she snapped, an echo of that worrying doubt sharpening her voice.

'All right, if that's the way you want to play it.' Hal dismissed her declaration with a shrug. 'But get one thing straight, lady. I'll bail you out this time, provided you keep to our agreement, but never again. After this you're on your own.'

'That suits me fine.' Thinking that the conversation was over, Laurel turned to pick up her bag. But Hal hadn't finished with her.

'We still have two months together ahead of us, so I suggest you curb that tongue of yours and try to be a bit more civil, because if you don't I swear I'll drop you right in whatever mess you're in and not give a damn whether you sink or swim. Is that understood?'

'Perfectly,' Laurel replied tightly, quailing inside at the ferocity of his tone, which was all the more disturbing because not once had he raised his voice. She was painfully aware of the way she had come perilously close to blowing the whole thing completely, risking her position and Jenny's future as she did so. Her heart ached as she pictured her small sister's white, drawn face. Suddenly Ashingby seemed a million miles away.

Lost in her unhappy thoughts, Laurel dimly heard Hal say, 'Well, we'd better be off,' and, moving like an automaton, she followed him blindly towards the door.

'Aren't you forgetting something?' Hal's mocking voice halted her in her tracks. As she turned a bewildered face to his he moved to pick up the envelope he had tossed on to the bed. 'After all the trouble you've gone to to get this, you surely aren't going to leave it behind, are you?'

Wordlessly Laurel snatched the proffered envelope and stuffed it into her bag. Just to touch it suddenly sickened her, its bulky thickness was a stabbing reminder of the deceit she was involved in. But that money was a lifeline to Jenny, her only hope, and she had to give her that hope, no matter what the cost to herself. Reluctantly she met Hal's eyes and saw the contempt that burned in them as he interpreted her reaction as one of childish petulance.

'I shall need to bank this.' The words came unevenly from lips stiff with the effort of holding back a cry of protest at the injustice of his thoughts. She had no right to complain at him thinking badly of her over such a little thing when what she was really doing was so very much worse.

'We'll pass the bank.' Hal's tone implied that he had anticipated her reaction. 'But you won't need to draw on it while you're living with me. I'll pay all your living expenses.'

'A kept woman!' Laurel commented sarcastically, her nerves still raw from the conflicting emotions that had assailed her.

'That's right,' Hal agreed imperturbably. 'But then you always were, weren't you?' And before Laurel had time to recover from the stab of that cynical comment he added, 'I've dealt with your hotel bill, so there's no reason for us to hang around.'

Laurel felt as if she had been run over by a steamroller, as if her life had been taken completely out of her hands and she was being manipulated as easily as a puppet on a string. The desire to dig in her heels, refuse to go through with this farce, was almost overwhelming. If she felt like this after less than an hour with Hal, how was she ever going to cope with the next two months?

Hal shot a swift, searching glance at her face. 'What's bugging you now?' he enquired drily.

'I resent the way you think you own me!' Laurel declared bitterly, and he gave a short, hard laugh.

'Resent away, lady. In my book I do own you—several thousand pounds' worth of you—and, believe me, I intend to get some return for my money.'

The bank was crowded and Laurel joined the shortest queue, silently wishing that she hadn't had to wait. Even this short delay gave her unwanted time to think. It would have been so much easier if she could have just walked up to a cashier and handed over the money with no time for doubts, for second thoughts. This should have been a wonderful moment, she should have been over the moon at the thought that she had kept her promise to Jenny, that she had found a way to ensure that her sister had the operation she needed so desperately, but her pleasure and relief were tainted by the way she had obtained the necessary money.

She could still back out. The queue shuffled forward slightly and a wave of near-panic swept over Laurel. Once she handed over the money and signed the deposit slip she was committed with no chance of going back, as guilty of fraud as any criminal. She would have taken Hal's money under false pretences—no, not taken it, because she had no intention of keeping the money. In her mind it was just a loan and somehow, though God knew how, she was determined that she would pay it back even if it took the rest of her life.

Her thoughts went to Hal outside in the car, a fact for which she was profoundly grateful; the prospect of him accompanying her and possibly seeing her name on the deposit slip had been too terrifying to contemplate. What if that *had* been genuine concern she had heard in his voice? It was one thing giving a cold, callous, manipulative man a taste of his own medicine by using him as he had once used her twin, quite another to impersonate his wife if he had ever, even in the slightest way, really cared for her. But then an echo of that arrogant, 'In my book I do own you,' sounded in her mind, sweeping away her doubts. No man could ever speak like that about a woman he had loved. The queue moved again and now she was actually at the counter. With her pulse thudding high up in her throat, Laurel reached into her bag and pulled out the envelope.

'Sign at the bottom, please.' The cashier pushed the deposit slip towards her and, her pen in her hand, Laurel stared at the figures on the form in blank consternation.

'I—I'm afraid there must be some mistake——'

The girl behind the counter shook her head. 'No mistake, I counted it very carefully.'

Her mind numb with shock, Laurel managed to scrawl a distinctly shaky signature, her thoughts not on what she was doing. Hal had given her not the half of the money she had asked for but all of it—every last penny—and before she had done anything to earn it! That was either the action of a very generous man or one supremely confident of his ability to keep her to her half of the bargain—most likely the latter, Laurel thought bitterly. Hal was no fool, even after so brief an acquaintance with him she knew that. He was the last person to pay out such a large sum of money without being sure of a good return on his investment.

It was as she put the receipt for her deposit into her bag that Laurel noticed Lorraine's purse, which she had been stunned to discover contained more than three hundred pounds and which she had intended to return to her sister's husband when she found him. She would do so now, she resolved. She had no right to any of it, it was quite separate from the money she was 'earning'. Fleetingly she also remembered the photograph of the fair-haired man she had believed to be Hal Rochester but who must have been just a friend of Lorraine's, unable to suppress a wish that he *had* been Hal. When compared with the real Hal's hard-hewn features, his face appeared almost kindly. How different her position might have been if he had been the man her twin had married.

Even from the opposite side of the road, Laurel could see the tension in Hal's body as he waited for her in the car, sitting stiffly erect in his seat, long brown fingers drumming restlessly on the steering wheel. What had he expected? That she would take the money and run? With a jolting sense of shock she realised just how easy it would have been to do exactly that. The bank had several entrances, two of them leading to completely different streets. It would have been perfectly possible to leave by one of them, unseen, never having deposited the money, and disappear without trace. She could feel those sea-blue eyes on her every inch of the way as she crossed the road, saw how Hal's hands ceased their restless movement as he waited silently as she got into the car.

'Business completed?' he enquired, and there was something different about his voice, a strange unevenness, almost as if he had never expected her to return, and, with the thought of how easy it would have been to escape from him still in her mind, Laurel had to wonder if he had given her all the money as some sort of test of her honesty. The suspicion stung furiously and, determined to prove such cynical suspicion unfounded, she put her hand on his arm to stop him as he moved to start the car.

'Just a minute,' she said quietly.

That brought those sea-coloured eyes swinging round to her, open suspicion now written all over Hal's face—suspicion and, for one fleeting moment, some other violent emotion that Laurel could not interpret before it was gone. In a second he was in control again, the closed shuttered look that slid down over his face making it look as if it was carved out of rock.

'Well?' he demanded harshly.

Laurel was reaching into her bag as he spoke. Opening Lorraine's purse, she pulled out the bundle of notes it contained and held it out towards Hal, who stared at it blankly.

'What's this?' he asked stonily.

'Your money.' Laurel's voice was low and uneven. Hal pushed the notes back at her with a violent gesture.

'What I gave you is yours.'

'Oh, but this isn't what you just gave me! It's—it's——' She broke off abruptly, knowing it was impossible to explain.

'Whatever it is, I don't want it,' growled Hal, his fingers closing over the steering wheel until the knuckles showed white.

'But I can't keep it!' Laurel protested. 'You've already given me everything I needed—I said I wouldn't take any more from you——'

'Keep it, damn you!' he snarled so viciously that she shrank away from him, jolting in her seat as he started the engine and swung the car out into the road with a savage movement, manoeuvring it down the narrow street, his eyes fixed on the road, driving with apparent total disregard for their safety but somehow managing to avoid hitting anything. As his hand moved to change gear Laurel's eyes were drawn to the tensing of muscle under the tanned skin of his arms and it was impossible not to recall how she had felt when those arms had closed round her on the previous night.

Was that how Lorraine had felt? she wondered, flinching at the pain that any thought of her twin always brought. Had her sister been swept off her feet by Hal, rushing into marriage with an intensity of emotion that denied all forms of logic? That hard-boned face with its heavy-lidded eyes and firm jawline was hardly approachable, it was true. It was the face of a man too used to getting his own way, too full of a brooding arrogance to ever let anyone really touch him, but Laurel felt she could understand why her sister had been drawn to him. Hadn't she herself felt the pull of his attraction from the moment she had become aware of the full power of those mesmeric eyes in the hotel bar?

'Hal's a man who knows what he wants,' Lorraine had said—and clearly he had wanted her sister. Laurel could well imagine how Hal had been drawn to her twin; Lorraine had always had men round her, like moths around a candle flame. A cold knife stabbed deep in her heart at the thought of that bright beauty now gone for ever.

But she was not Lorraine. She had little experience of the male sex, nothing that would prepare her for a man of Hal Rochester's type. Privately Laurel admitted that because of Jenny she had been deprived of the normal adolescent's freedom to play the field, flirt, enjoy herself, and by doing so learn the intricacies of male-female relationships. She felt no resentment towards the little girl, if she had it all to do again she would behave in exactly the same way, but she was a woman, after all, and the years since her parents' deaths had been long, difficult, and very often lonely. The few boyfriends she had dated had been put off by the simple fact of Jenny's existence, and in a way who could blame them? Few young men in their twenties would want to take on the responsibility of a six-year-old sister, no matter how they felt about Laurel herself.

They were driving along the coast road now, still travelling at a dangerous speed, and Laurel was glad of Hal's intent absorption as her thoughts went to her small sister, so far away and yet always with her, inside her heart. What was Jenny doing now? Sleeping probably; the drugs the doctor gave her kept her almost permanently drowsy. But in a little while the nurses would come to give her a bed-bath—and for only the second time since the accident Laurel would not be there to help them. Barbara had been wonderful, letting her take all the time she needed to be with her sister—as she had raised no objection to her staying in Nunham, simply telling her that her job would be waiting for her when she got back. Laurel sighed, thinking longingly of that time when she would be free to be herself once again, then was jolted back to the present as the car swung suddenly right and up a small, sloping drive to draw to a halt outside a large, white-painted house.

A faint gasp broke from Laurel's lips. It was not so much the house which, on further inspection, proved to be two semi-detached houses combined into one, that caused her reaction but its situation, perched high on a cliff top with a garden which on one side dropped sheer down to the sea. In the silence she could hear the waves crashing against the rocks below. Completely forgetting the restraint there had been between them, she turned to Hal in spontaneous delight.

'What a wonderful place? You must love living here.'

'You like it?' Hal's tone implied doubt as to her sincerity.

'I love it!' Laurel responded enthusiastically, longing to get out of the car and walk to the cliff edge, feel the wind in her hair, the spray on her face.

'It's nothing like my house in London,' Hal said slowly, his eyes intent on her face. 'It's very isolated. I like it that way, but it can get very lonely at times.'

And now Laurel knew the reason for that sceptical tone of voice. *Lorraine* would have hated this place for its loneliness, for its isolation from the gaiety and excitement of the busy social life she had always wanted. She felt as if a great chasm had suddenly opened up underneath her feet, leaving her balanced precariously above it so that the slightest false move could send her plunging downwards to destruction. It was one thing to let Hal believe she was Lorraine in the heat of her first confrontation with him, quite another to maintain that pretence in the intimate atmosphere of his home. There were so many things that a wife would know about her husband—and vice versa—so many small, personal things she knew nothing about. She didn't even know if he took sugar in his coffee!

To cover her confusion, Laurel got out of the car as swiftly as she could, welcoming the blast of air that blew in from the sea to cool her burning cheeks. This was going to be so much more difficult than she had ever anticipated. It was on those small, insignificant details that her chance of helping Jenny would stand or fall.

When Hal unlocked the door a black whirlwind in the shape of Jet the labrador flung itself on him, tail wagging furiously. He quietened swiftly at a word of command and turned his sleek black head in Laurel's direction, his ears pricked in interest. Automatically Laurel held out her hand to him, letting him sniff it thoroughly before attempting to pat him.

'He's a fine animal,' she said, keeping her tone carefully neutral. Lorraine had never shared her longing for a dog of her own. But she couldn't prevent a smile from surfacing when a long pink tongue licked her lovingly.

That smile had the strangest effect on Hal. For a long moment he stared at her, his eyes narrowed, as if he couldn't believe she was real. Then abruptly he bent to pick up her case.

'I'll take this upstairs,' he said, his voice rough-edged. At the foot of the staircase he paused, looking back at Laurel. 'A friend gave me Jet,' he added sardonically. 'He kept me from being too lonely when you'd gone.'

If she believed that, she would turn and run, unable to live with what she'd done, Laurel thought to herself. But the black cynicism of Hal's tone told her that he hadn't meant what he'd said, in fact he'd meant her to understand quite the opposite.

Left alone, she turned to the nearest door leading off the hall and opened it, finding that it led into a room that had her standing still in sheer delight. When the two houses had been converted into one, the living-room and dining-room of one had been combined into this huge room that stretched the length of that side of the house. Large glass patio doors took up almost all of one wall, giving full benefit of the magnificent view of the cliffs and the sea and flooding the room with light. The furnishings were simple, almost stark, two leather-covered settees, each big enough to seat four people, taking pride of place. The walls were cream, the floorboards sanded and varnished and covered by large, brightly patterned rugs. In the centre of one wall was an open fireplace flanked on either side by bookcases filled to overflowing.

It was an essentially masculine room with curtains in deep rust and brown to match the main tones of the rugs; there was no hint of any feminine influence, and, much more important, there was nothing in the room to remind Laurel of her twin, no ornament or painting her sister might have chosen. But then Hal had said that Lorraine had never seen Highcliff. Laurel let her breath escape in a great sigh of relief. She couldn't have borne to live with a daily reminder of the loss that was still too painful for her to really believe that it had happened.

When Hal returned he had changed out of his denims and T-shirt into a pair of dark grey trousers and a silvery grey shirt, worn casually open at the neck, but even in the more elegant clothes he still retained that wild pirate look Laurel had found so compelling at their first meeting. It had the same effect on her now, destroying her composure and making her heart thud uncomfortably. If they had met in other circumstances—— She clamped down hard on the weak thought before it had time to form. There could be no other circumstances, and even if they had met in some very different way Hal would still be Hal, a callous, arrogant, ruthless man, the sort of person she would detest even if there hadn't been the added impetus of his treatment of Lorraine to make her dislike him before she had met him.

'I thought we'd go into Marborough,' Hal was saying casually. 'We could do some shopping.'

'Shopping?' Laurel echoed faintly, unsure that she had heard right. 'What sort of shopping?'

'You need some clothes,' he pointed out. 'Marborough's not London, of course, but there are some decent——'

'Now wait a minute!' Laurel broke in on him. 'Are you implying——'

'I'm implying nothing, I'm telling you—you need some clothes, and the sooner the better. I can't have my wife looking like some charity case.'

There it was again—'my wife'—the possessive tone grating on Laurel's raw nerves.

'I can't afford any clothes,' she declared defiantly, trying to assert herself, to rid herself of the feeling that she was only a puppet, one whose strings Hal held firmly in his hands.

'But I can,' was the imperturbable response.

'But I can't let you pay for my clothes!' She'd taken enough from him already; even allowing for the fact that he was the most hateful man she had ever met, her conscience wouldn't let her take any more.

'That never bothered you before,' he replied in the coldly reasonable voice she had already come to know and fear. 'What makes this time so different?'

'You know what makes it different! You've been generous enough already—I can't take any more of your money.'

'Generous?' Hal repeated the word in a low voice, looking, just for a split second, as if she had struck him in the face. Then, abruptly, his mood changed. 'Your sudden acquisition of a conscience is quite amazing,' he went on, dark irony lacing his tone. 'If you intended to surprise me, you have, but right now it's totally irrelevant. You agreed to act as my wife again, and the least you can do is look the part. I am buying you some new clothes and you are going to wear them if I have to dress you in them myself. Besides, I'm expecting guests next week. I do not intend that they should think I'm too mean to give my wife a decent clothes allowance.'

Laurel heard his words with a sense of shock. In one respect these unexpected guests would make things easier because their presence would inevitably mean that she and Hal would have to spend less time alone together. But it would also mean that there would be other people to convince that she was Lorraine, and she didn't know if she could do it, particularly when she had no idea how well her sister had known these people. The days ahead were going to be fraught with complications. Already she felt as if she was balanced precariously on a high tightrope, and the mention of the visitors brought with it a picture of Lorraine, alive and well, sharing a life and friends with Hal, which was savagely destructive to her peace of mind.

'Do I take it that this silence means you've decided to see sense?' Hal's voice broke in on her thoughts. 'If it helps to appease your newly acquired conscience, you can consider the clothes as part of your living expenses. We agreed I'd pay those while you were here, didn't we?'

'Yes—yes, we did.'

Laurel was having difficulty imposing any order on her thoughts through the multitude of disturbing emotions that swirled inside her head. There was the pain that was always just below the surface when she thought of her twin, a stab of anger at the thought of the life Lorraine had led with this domineering man, the sting of the realisation, once again, that Hal's offer to buy his 'wife' clothes had been made simply to ensure that she did not disgrace him in front of his friends, not from any generous impulse to please her as a person. But mixed with those was another feeling, one that had come with the thought of the life Hal and Lorraine had lived before she had even known he existed, and to which she couldn't put a name. In other circumstances she might have called it jealousy, but she could see no reason to feel any such emotion now. What was there in her twin's relationship with her husband that she could possibly envy?

'We'll leave in an hour.' Hal had evidently taken her words as agreement. 'So why don't you go upstairs and unpack?' Blue eyes skimmed over her body and once more he frowned his distaste for the blue dress. 'And I suggest you change into something a little more presentable—if there is anything more stylish among that deplorable collection of clothes you've brought with you.'

CHAPTER FOUR

LAUREL'S first thought on her return to Highcliff was that she had to find some way of phoning Jenny. Visiting time would already have started and the sister on the ward had promised that she would take the portable telephone to Jenny's bed if Laurel rang. Although she knew Barbara would be with the little girl she was desperate to talk to her sister herself. They had never been apart for more than a few hours before, and the need to hear Jenny's voice was so intense it was like a physical pain. But how could she ring the hospital with Hal in the house?

Luckily at that moment Hal announced that he was taking Jet for a walk along the beach.

'The poor beast's been cooped up in the house all day, he needs some exercise. I'll be about an hour, OK?'

Laurel's nod was abstracted, her mind far away, with Jenny. Her need left no room for caution.

'Can I use the phone while you're out?' she blurted out hastily. Hal's sudden stillness, his silence, worried her. 'I'll keep a record of the calls I make and what they cost,' she added unevenly.

Hal's head went back slightly as if something she'd said had shocked him. 'No need for that,' he said gruffly. 'Use it any time you like—don't bother to ask.'

Laurel watched him leave, the dog at his heels, and knew a pang of longing to be free to go with him. The beach outside seemed to call to her; she would have loved to run along its soft, smooth sand, feel the wind in her hair, and perhaps kick off her shoes and paddle in the sea. With a brusque shake of her head she drove such thoughts from her mind. She wasn't here to enjoy herself, but to help Jenny—and Jenny would be waiting for her call.

When she made her way upstairs twenty minutes later, Laurel felt easier in her mind for the first time since Hal had confronted her outside the hotel. Jenny had sounded brighter than ever before, though she still complained that her back hurt her constantly. She had been rebellious at the thought of her sister staying away for longer than she had expected, but she had soon come round when she realised that Laurel's absence meant that she was keeping her promise to ensure that Jenny would dance again as soon as possible. The excitement that crept into her voice when she realised that the vital operation would take place as soon as it could be arranged lifted Laurel's spirits. No matter what she had to put up with, it was all worth it just to hear Jenny taking an interest in things again. Nothing could be more important than that the little girl should get well again—and suddenly that seemed very much closer.

Hal had carried the clothes they had bought during the afternoon up to her room and Laurel began to unpack the bags and boxes, hanging the dresses, skirts and blouses in the wardrobe, her mind going back over the time they had spent in Marborough, recalling her numbed shock at the amount of clothes Hal had insisted on buying for her, far more than she needed for the two months allotted to her.

In other circumstances the shopping trip could have been a delight, an escape from the penny-pinching days of buying only what she really needed—and then only if there was any money left after paying the bills. To spend an afternoon in an exclusive shop, trying on anything and everything that took her fancy, selecting the things she liked without a thought for what it cost, should have seemed like a dream come true, but the ordeal of facing Hal's appraising eyes in every garment she tried on, the knowledge that it was his money that was paying for the growing pile of clothes she had chosen, tainted the whole experience, taking all the pleasure from it.

And there had been that other, agonising moment when, encouraged by the salesgirl, she had been persuaded into trying on a dress that was new in that day, its style in the very height of fashion. Laurel's hands tightened on the blouse she had unpacked, crushing its silky material heedlessly. When she had turned to look at herself in the changing-room mirror the image she saw had reminded her so forcefully of Lorraine as she had looked when she had left the house to drive Jenny to school on that fateful journey from which she had never returned that Laurel had swayed weakly, leaning against the wall for support. After that she had insisted on trying on only the more classical styles which were genuinely more to her own personal taste and had stubbornly resisted all attempts to persuade her to consider anything more modern.

Her movements abrupt and jerky, Laurel hurried through the rest of the unpacking until there was only one large box left. Her hands stilled as she touched it, remembering what it contained.

'I want something special,' Hal had instructed the salesgirl. 'Something suitable for evening wear. We have some friends coming up from London——'

'I know just the thing,' the girl had responded, and she had produced a dress that had made Laurel catch her breath, her eyes widening in stunned delight.

It was the sort of dress she had always dreamed of wearing: drifting, almost ethereal layers of chiffon in muted shades of green, the palest almost white, the darkest a perfect match for Laurel's eyes, the soft folds of material falling from a square bodice with shoestring straps. Laurel knew she didn't have to try it on—it would be perfect, she knew that just by looking at it, but she also knew that she could never accept it. French design showed in every inch of the dress and the price would mirror that fact.

'Try it on,' Hal suggested persuasively.

Laurel wanted to shake her head, to tell him that she couldn't let him buy her such a dress. It was the sort of dress a man would buy for the woman he loved and, tormented by her uneasy conscience, she knew she could never accept it from Hal. But her body refused to obey her as she reached out and touched the soft material, unaware of the longing that was written clearly on her face.

'Try it on, Lori,' Hal repeated, and a strange unevenness in his voice drew her eyes to his face, catching the swift frown that made her fearful of disobeying him.

The dress fitted perfectly as she had known it would, and for a long moment she stared disbelievingly at her own reflection in the mirror, swaying slightly so that the delicate material swirled sensuously round her like a pale mist. She started nervously as the curtains were pulled back and Hal appeared in the opening, his eyes narrowing as he took in the soft curve of pleasure on her lips, her glowing eyes.

Slowly Laurel turned to face him, meeting his appraising gaze with a new confidence. She knew that never before had she looked so good, so feminine, and she felt a thrill of excitement as she watched his expression change, warming to a look so frankly sensuous and approving that it was almost a physical caress. His response was so unlike the cool approach with which he had greeted every other garment she had chosen that Laurel reacted instinctively, smiling her delight straight into those blue eyes that now seemed so dark they were almost black.

'That's perfect,' he said huskily. 'We'll take it.'

The sound of his voice broke the spell that had held her silent.

'Hal, no!' she protested unthinkingly, and Hal leaned forward to lay one long finger across her lips to silence her.

'Hal, *yes*,' he corrected softly. 'Do you know,' he went on in a low voice meant for Laurel's ears only, 'that's the first time you've used my name since you arrived. It's amazing what a few new clothes can do to change a woman's mind.'

Laurel felt sick. Hal's cynical assumption that she had changed her attitude to him on purely materialistic grounds stung more sharply, coming as it did after those few seconds of unity they had shared before he spoke.

Still, what had she expected? she asked herself now as she shook out the folds of the green dress and hung it on a hanger. Lorraine had said that the only thing Hal cared about was money, so naturally he would judge everyone else on those terms.

With all the clothes put away there was still half an hour to fill before Hal returned, and Laurel decided to have a shower. She felt hot and sticky after the heat of the day and the tensions of the afternoon had left her jaded and lacking in energy. A shower would refresh her.

In the bathroom she found fresh towels laid ready and—she stood still in shock, staring at the collection of toiletries, soap, bath gel, talcum powder, even body lotion arranged where she could not miss them and clearly intended for her use. The distinctive white and gold packaging was easily recognisable and she didn't need to read the labels to know that they were French, the sort of thing that was well beyond the reach of her limited finances. Hal had had hardly any time to prepare for her arrival and yet he had thought to provide these small luxuries. Her conscience stabbed uncomfortably at the thought. That was the gesture of a man who wanted to please—to please his *wife*, she forced herself to admit, knowing the toiletries had been bought for

Lorraine—and that didn't fit with the image of the ruthless, uncaring monster she had built up in her mind.

She wouldn't use them! She couldn't! She would make do with her own far less luxurious items. But how would she explain to Hal the reasons why she had rejected his gift? As she glanced again at the beautifully packaged containers, temptation overcame her resolve. She could never afford anything like this for herself——

But once she had stepped under the shower and begun to soap herself all over the fragrance released by the warmth of the water brought a sudden rush of memory as she recognised the scent as the one Lorraine had been wearing the last time she had seen her twin. Tears welled up in her eyes, then overflowed and joined the water cascading down her face, and she clasped her arms around her body as if to hold herself together as the pain threatened to tear her in two. But a moment later another thought had her freezing in shock, sending a shiver running through her that even the warmth of the shower could not dispel.

These perfumes had not been bought by chance, perhaps on the recommendation of some salesgirl, but had been selected carefully with one particular woman in mind—a woman to whom they were as personal as her signature. They had been chosen for Lorraine, intended to give her pleasure. In the brief time between her agreement to Hal's conditions and his arrival at the hotel to collect her he had taken the trouble to find such a personal gift. Was that the action of a man who cared nothing for his wife, who treated her only as a possession, never having truly loved her? Or were the perfumes, like the clothes, simply intended to make sure that she made the right impression on his friends? She had to believe that was so, needed desperately to believe it, because she couldn't go on with this deception if she ever suspected that Hal had truly cared for Lorraine—

and she *had* to go on with it if Jenny were to have any chance of walking again.

Laurel reached up and turned on the shower more powerfully, letting the water pound down on her head until she was incapable of thought, but still couldn't rid herself of the feeling of being a small, frightened fly caught in an elaborate and luxurious spider's web with its strands gathering closer round her with every minute that passed.

It was a long time before she felt calm enough to return to the bedroom, but at last, with a thin cotton robe her only covering, she pushed open the door, freezing in shock as she saw the dark figure standing beside the window.

'What are you doing here?' she demanded, her voice high-pitched and sharp, her hands clutching nervously at the fronts of her robe which showed a disturbing tendency to slip revealingly.

Hal's dark eyebrows drew together ominously, but his voice had the coolly reasonable tone she hated as he answered, 'I've every right to be here. This happens to be my bedroom too.'

'Your bedroom!' Laurel's head went back in shock, her eyes widening until they were deep green pools in a face that was suddenly drained of every trace of colour.

In the brief time she had spent in it she had taken very little notice of the room Hal had allocated to her, other than to realise that some of the strong colours of the living-room had been used again upstairs. Now those colours appeared so uncompromisingly masculine that she cursed herself for not having realised before. She had put her clothes, old and new, in the large wardrobe that had stood open and empty, but there was another of similar size beyond the dressing-table. Unwillingly her eyes went to the double bed that seemed suddenly to have grown until it appeared to her numbed brain that it almost filled the room.

'I'm not sleeping——'

'Oh, but you are,' Hal broke in swiftly. 'You're here to act as my *wife*. No one's going to believe we're happily married if we sleep in separate rooms.'

'But we're not!—happily married, I mean,' Laurel amended hastily, panic-stricken by what she had almost revealed. Hal's mouth twisted cynically.

'Maybe not, but that's the impression I want to give— so you'll sleep here, whether you like it or not.'

'I won't! I can't!' Sharing Hal's life was one thing, sharing his bed quite another.

'Why so shy, my lovely?' he questioned silkily, his eyes moving slowly over her body, lingering deliberately on the soft flesh, still pink from the warmth of the shower, revealed at the neck of her robe. 'We did live together for four months, remember?'

The swift darkening of his eyes set Laurel's heart thudding. His gaze seemed to strip away the protection of the robe as effectively as if he had torn it from her, and instinctively she shrank back, fiery colour burning in her cheeks. The few brief relationships she had had with men in the past had never moved beyond the point of friendship, she hadn't had the time or the freedom to take things any further, and so nothing had prepared her for the devastating effect of being alone with a man as virile and attractive as Hal Rochester in the intimate confines of a bedroom—*his* bedroom!

His hand closed over her shoulder, hard fingers digging into her skin as he drew her nearer, then bent his head to brush a light kiss across her forehead, his lips warm and soft and surprisingly gentle. One arm slid around her waist, holding her easily while the other hand lifted her chin so that her lips met his with an inevitability that seemed as natural as breathing. Laurel felt she had lost all will of her own, her fear seeming to have flown, replaced by a searing wave of desire that left her shaken, leaning against his hard strength for support, and hazed her mind with a golden mist.

'We don't have to be strangers, Lori,' Hal whispered against her lips, then his mouth fastened on hers again with a pressure that made her senses reel. Unknowingly she was clinging to him, her hands tangling in his hair, revelling in the pressure of his body against hers, the warmth of his fingers on her skin as they slid under the robe. She was unaware of the fact that he was drawing her unresistingly towards the bed, covering her face with kisses as he lowered her gently on to it, his hands efficiently disposing of the robe as he did so, until the cool touch of the air on her heated flesh brought her swiftly back to sanity.

'No!'

In a panic Laurel struggled to sit up, her hands pushing desperately but ineffectually at Hal's chest. She couldn't let this happen, not with this man, this hateful, callous creature who had treated her sister so badly. Frantically she groped for her robe, but failed to find it, and in a fury of embarrassment crossed her arms protectively across her breasts.

'No?' Hal questioned mockingly, trailing burning kisses along the line of her throat. To Laurel's horror she felt herself weakening again, felt flames of excitement flicker in her blood. She had to put a stop to this! Hal's lips moved lower.

'I said no!' Somehow Laurel found a strength she didn't know she possessed and twisted away from him, her hand finally finding her robe which she gathered frantically to her, forcing her arms into its sleeves, careless of the fact that it was inside out as Hal straightened slowly and turned to face her.

He stood only a few feet away from her, his arms folded across his powerful chest, terrifyingly dark and threatening as he towered over her. His expression was a mixture of suppressed anger and icy contempt which made Laurel's stomach twist in fear. But what made matters far worse was the fact that, from the moment his hands had left her body, she had felt an agonising sense of loss that had now formed itself into a tight knot of frustration deep in the pit of her stomach. What was happening to her? Had she really not wanted him to stop? Had she actually *wanted* this man to make love to her?

'OK, lady, you've made your point.' Hal's tone was dangerous, his eyes sea-coloured chips of ice. 'But let's get one thing straight. I want a wife in every sense of the word, not just someone pretty to have around the place, and a wife is what I'm going to have.'

'A wife in name only!' Laurel flung at him. 'You made the conditions.'

'Well, now I'm changing them,' he parried smoothly. 'From the minute I saw you in that green dress I knew——' He broke off abruptly, appearing to reconsider what he had been about to say. 'I realised that you were getting your money far too easily.'

With a sickening lurch of her stomach Laurel recalled the moment Hal had pulled back the changing-room curtain, the sensual appreciation that had darkened his eyes, and her breath caught in her throat. Had he taken her own smile as recognition of the desire he had felt then? Had he thought she was encouraging, even inviting, the sort of intimacies she had just narrowly escaped?

'Don't tell me you didn't enjoy what we were doing just now,' Hal's voice broke in on her whirling thoughts. 'I'm not blind or a fool—I know when a woman's responding——'

'What we were doing just now'—but to Hal that 'we' meant himself and *Lorraine*, and there was one very vital difference between Laurel and her twin. Hal wanted Lorraine in his bed, his wife, a woman he had made love to before, but Laurel had no experience of such matters, had never met a man she cared enough about to even consider sleeping with him.

Hal's change of tactics altered everything. His conditions were no longer ones she could meet—but she was already committed. The money was in the bank—in the name of Laurel Grahame—and at the hospital things had been set in motion. The American surgeon would have been contacted; Jenny knew that the operation was to take place very soon. Could she call a halt now, take things back to the way they had been before with the prospect of her young sister being confined to a wheelchair and no hope of finding the money she needed? A cold hand squeezed her heart as the image of Jenny over the past weeks, pale and miserable, in constant pain, floated before her eyes. She had been prepared to do anything to give the little girl a chance of a happy future—but this——!

'Won't that delay the divorce you want?' she tried desperately, saying the first thing that came into her head that might possibly make him change his mind.

Hal shrugged indifferently. 'It might be worth it. I consider it a pretty fair bargain.'

'Fair!' Laurel's voice cracked on the word. 'How can you call it fair? You don't know what you're asking!'

'Anyone would think you were a virgin on her wedding night!' he exclaimed in exasperation. 'Come on, lady. You know you'll enjoy it—we both will. You must have felt the electricity between us, you can't deny that.'

Laurel felt the colour drain from her face as she recalled the way she had responded to him only moments before. For the first time in her life she had known what sexual desire truly meant. She had been putty in Hal's hands, rational thought driven away by the burning need that even now still made her body ache in frustration at the abrupt ending she had imposed on it. She would have said that it was impossible to feel such passion for a man she didn't know or like—a man she hated—but the fire

Hal had lit in her had driven away all other considerations.

Was this how Lorraine had felt? Had her sister too been swept off her feet by this man, rushing into marriage with an intensity of emotion that denied all forms of logic? Her eyes slid to Hal, her gaze travelling slowly over the hard-boned handsomeness of his face, the wide, powerful shoulders, the narrow waist and hips. She had never really appreciated any man physically before, but now she couldn't help wondering what it would feel like to have that magnificent body beside her in bed. Suddenly she knew that the problem would not be one of forcing herself to allow his lovemaking but quite the opposite. She had the intuitive and totally unwelcome conviction that if Hal really made love to her she would never want him to stop.

But could she ever allow that to happen? Could she let this man make love to her without being discovered at once? Was it true that a man could always tell if it was the first time for a woman? When they were teenagers, Lorraine had laughed at the idea, declaring it was just a myth men put about, that nowadays it was impossible for anyone to know if a girl was a virgin or not.

Lorraine! Laurel shuddered as she realised the way her thoughts had been heading. She could never pretend to be her sister—*Hal's wife*—in his bed. The deceit she was ensnared in already was bad enough, the thought of taking it any further sickened her. But she was in a cleft stick. If she didn't agree to Hal's terms it meant abandoning Jenny.

Suddenly Hal swung round to face her, his eyes very dark in a face that seemed strained and drawn, deepening the harsh lines around his nose and mouth.

'Do you know what you're doing to me?' he demanded roughly. 'I hate who you are, what you are, yet now, when you're here with me like this——'

His eyes went to the front of Laurel's robe, still gaping open, and hurriedly she drew it closer round her, her hands fumbling with the belt.

'It's all I can do to keep my hands off you. I want you, and I'm damned sure you want me every bit as much—but there's no future for us that way. Perhaps we can survive these two months, and maybe by then I'll have got you out of my system.'

Laurel's head reeled as if his words had been actual physical blows. She could scarcely believe that she had heard what he was saying correctly. Oh, Lorraine, Lorraine, what sort of a monster did you marry? Only now could she fully understand her twin's bitterness.

'You're disgusting!'

'What's wrong, Lori? Don't you like it when someone else does the taking? Don't you think it's your turn to start giving? You took enough from me in the past, damn you! I'm only asking for a little in return. What else did you expect? You came strolling back into my life because I have something you want, then you have the nerve to object when I want something in return. Well, hard luck! You used me and now I'm using you!'

'Used!' Only the struggle she was having to get any words out prevented Laurel from lashing out verbally. How could a man who had treated Lorraine the way he had accuse her twin of using *him*? Her merciless conscience stabbed at her with the reminder that *she* was the one who was using anyone, driving her into reckless speech, heedless of the possible consequences. 'And you think that money's sufficient compensation for what you want?'

'If it wasn't you'd never have agreed to the deal,' Hal returned callously. 'You could have held out for more; I'd probably have paid it.'

'I didn't realise your motivation was quite so bestial!' she spat at him. 'You talk as if I was some particularly nasty form of infection—something that has to be lived through until you develop an immunity! What is it you want from me? Some form of aversion therapy to cure you?'

It was as she flung the last words at him that she realised exactly what she'd said. *I* and *me*—she had been thinking of Lorraine at the start, but somewhere something had changed. She hadn't even been pretending to be Lorraine for Jenny's sake, her feelings were in such turmoil that she was past knowing how to act for the best for her little sister. Hal's words had hurt her savagely—and the pain she had felt was all her own.

Hal laughed suddenly, a cold, hard sound with no humour in it.

'I'd forgotten just what a shrew you could be. Perhaps aversion therapy's the right term after all. Keep this up, Lori, and two months will be more than enough.'

'You still expect me to stay after what you've just said?' Laurel stammered incredulously.

'Why not? Nothing's changed. You were prepared to come and live with me provided I paid you enough—I'm still prepared to let you have the money—more than you asked for, if that's what it takes.'

'*No!*' In a haze of disordered thoughts, one thing was clear in Laurel's mind. She had forced herself to swallow her doubts about the arrangement as it stood—she couldn't profit by it herself. The money for Jenny was all she wanted.

'No?' Hal actually took a step backwards in surprise, shock and consternation flashing across his face. But a moment later he had shrugged off his confusion. 'Well, if that's the way you want it—but I retract none of my conditions. This is still purely a business deal.'

'Payment for services rendered,' Laurel muttered bitterly, able at last, in this tenuous calm, to think more clearly, to remember Jenny and how much this meant to her. She was frankly stunned to find that, in spite of everything, Hal was still offering to let her keep the money. But he had been wrong when he had said that nothing had changed. There was still the new condition, one that she didn't believe she could fulfil.

She felt drained and limp with exhaustion and yet, strangely enough, she felt better too. It was like being in the calm after a violent storm when the oppressive tension hanging threateningly in the air had eased. Because, in a way, what Hal had said made things easier. His obvious lack of feeling—other than physical—where she or, rather, Lorraine, was concerned meant that she need have little compunction about deceiving him. He had proved himself the heartless man Lorraine had described. All he wanted was a body on which to appease his lust, and the mind and heart inside that body were quite simply irrelevant. True, the body he actually lusted after was Lorraine's, but when her own body was as similar to her sister's as any other human being's could possibly be, he could hardly consider himself unfairly treated.

Except, of course, that she was no longer sure that the desire she had experienced earlier was strong enough to overcome the repugnance she now felt for him—and if he made love to her, wouldn't he know, once and for all, that she was not Lorraine?

'And—your new condition?' Laurel had to struggle to get the words out.

'I still want you, Lori,' Hal replied curtly. 'Nothing's changed that.'

In the back of her mind Laurel could hear her sister's voice echoing his words. 'Hal's the sort of man who knows what he wants and when he finds it he acts— fast.' Now she believed she could understand just how her sister had felt, why she had let herself be steam- rollered into a marriage that was a mistake from the start. Trying to fight Hal Rochester was like trying to cope with a floodtide using a seaside bucket.

'You're nothing if not blunt,' she said shakily, trying to gain precious time in which to think.

'I don't deal in half-truths. I agreed to pay for a wife and a wife is what I intend to have, otherwise the deal's off.'

'Don't honour what you want with the name of a wife!' Laurel spat at him, too preoccupied with her own quandary to care that she sounded cold and hard, quite the opposite of the terrifyingly vulnerable way she was actually feeling. 'A wife would want much more than you're offering! It's just a body that you're paying for!'

Hal's head went back, his eyes narrowing swiftly, but not before she had seen the sudden flare of emotion in them, the flash of—anger? amazement? admiration?— she was beyond guessing which.

'If that's the way you want to play it,' he declared grimly. 'And right now you come pretty expensive, my lovely.'

Laurel's temper boiled over once and for all. 'Is that the only way you can get a woman in your bed—by buying her?'

Hal's face darkened ominously. 'I don't need to buy my women,' he snarled. 'That's a problem I've only ever had with my wife. Oh, don't look so horrified, lady. I don't plan on rape. I've never forced a woman yet and I don't intend to start with you. I want to take you to bed, true, but I'll not fight you. You'll share my home and my bed—the rest will come in its own good time.'

His easy confidence was the last straw for Laurel.

'Never!' she cried vehemently. 'I wouldn't sleep with you if you were the last man on earth!'

To her amazement a slow smile curved Hal's lips, but then she noticed that the lightening of his expression wasn't reflected in his eyes, they remained frighteningly cold and hard.

'Then I know you better than you know yourself, lady,' he drawled lazily. 'I had you in my arms just now—

I felt your response. You can say what you like, but I know things aren't the way they used to be. If you'd just stop fighting you'd see how easy it will be to earn your money.'

But Laurel barely heard the last taunt; Hal's earlier words had struck her with the force of a blow. 'The way they used to be'—that had been when Lorraine was alive. Things could never be how they used to be again. A low moan escaped her and she swayed on her feet.

'Are you all right?' Hal's voice was suddenly sharp with concern. 'Lori, what is it?'

He reached out to take her arm to support her, and instinctively Laurel flinched away from his touch. The sea-blue eyes darkened swiftly.

'For God's sake, Lori, don't look at me like that!' he exclaimed harshly. 'I'm not going to hurt you—just tell me what's wrong.'

If only she could! For a moment she was tempted. If ever there was a time to tell him, it was now, when the hostility between them had lessened, when there was a chance of him listening to her. But fear paralysed her and the moment was lost.

'I'm—tired,' she said slowly, the dull, flat tones of her voice reinforcing the simple statement. And it was true, she felt exhausted, every muscle in her body aching with the tension she had endured.

'And hungry, too, no doubt,' Hal added with a glance at his watch. 'It's hours since we ate.'

The sudden change in his voice was shocking. The hard, aggressive note had gone, leaving it soft and disturbingly attractive. Laurel almost expected to find that Hal had vanished and someone else had taken his place.

'Why don't you get dressed while I see what Mrs Tillotson's left for dinner?'

Taking her stunned silence for agreement, he headed for the door, then abruptly turned back.

'About that other thing,' he said quietly. 'If it worries you so much we'll leave it till you're settled in. I'm not a complete brute and, as you said, in a way we're really strangers to each other.'

Laurel stood frozen for several minutes after he had gone, staring at the door that had swung to behind him, unable to move because her mind felt numbed with shock. Just when she had thought all was lost, Hal had offered her a reprieve—in the same way as, on the previous night, he had unhesitatingly offered the money she needed, believing her to be Lorraine. The 'conditions' had come later. She had believed it was pointless to consider right or wrong when dealing with Hal Rochester, thinking him a man who lived by his own amoral set of rules, that nothing she might do would touch him. But the consideration he had shown just now didn't fit with her image of a man totally without any finer feelings.

A sensation like the trickle of icy water down her spine made her shiver convulsively as she recalled the accusations of selfishness Hal had flung at her. They had been meant for Lorraine, so had her sister been as innocent in the break-up of her marriage as she had led Laurel to believe? If Hal had ever cared for her twin, in however small a way, then this deception could hurt him savagely if he ever discovered the truth. But without the deceit and the money she had obtained through it Jenny would lose her chance of a happy and healthy future.

In her mind Laurel pictured Jenny as she had been just a few weeks ago, at her sixth birthday party, her eyes alight with laughter, a crêpe-paper hat perched precariously on the glowing red hair, her slim body for once totally feminine in a pretty white dress instead of the jeans and T-shirts that were her usual choice of clothing.

No one who had seen the child's joyful face as she tap-danced her way round the flat's small living-room, unable to keep her feet still, responding instinctively to the music on the radio, could ever doubt that to deprive Jenny of the chance of ever dancing again was the cruellest blow fate could ever have dealt her, especially when Jenny had already suffered the devastating loss of both her parents when she was still just a toddler. Surely anyone who had seen that total absorption, the contrast between the bright elf of her birthday and the child who now lay in a hospital bed, would believe that in this case the end justified any means used to bring it about.

But Hal had never seen Jenny, didn't even know she existed, and in spite of all her arguments the cold feeling still lingered even after she had pulled on her clothes, and as Laurel slowly made her way downstairs doubt and uncertainty enclosed her heart in a wall of ice.

CHAPTER FIVE

'YOU MUST be Mrs Tillotson.'

Hal's housekeeper surprised Laurel. She had expected a stout, grey-haired, elderly lady, but the woman she met in the kitchen the next morning was in her early thirties at most, with neat dark hair and an open, smiling face.

'I'm—Lauri——' She hesitated over the name, reluctant to use her sister's and settling for the shortened version Hal used which would cover both hers and Lorraine's.

Mrs Tillotson nodded. 'Mr Rochester told me,' she replied easily, making Laurel wonder just what explanation Hal had given her. 'But please call me Jan, everyone else does.'

'Jan it is, then,' Laurel agreed readily, finding the housekeeper's friendly manner a relief after the pressure and strain of being with Hal—though, after the confrontation in the bedroom, last night had been surprisingly easy.

'I've been thinking,' Hal had said when she finally joined him in the kitchen. 'I think we'd better start again. This thing's never going to work if we both keep raking up the past. You were right when you said I was a stranger. We've never really known each other. But if we *were* strangers we'd behave better than this, wouldn't we?'

The wry amusement in his eyes was dangerously appealing, and Laurel felt her stomach twist into tight, uncomfortable knots. They *were* strangers, but Hal must never know that. And how could they start again when the lie she was living must always come between them? She was shocked to find how much she wanted that new beginning—but a real, honest fresh start, not just the temporary truce Hal was offering. But Hal had said that only his wife would get the money he was paying her, and after all that had happened between them he would never even consider helping her if she told him the truth. It was too late for honesty now; it would only bring the destruction of all her hopes for Jenny.

'We'll take it one step at a time,' Hal was saying, his tone carefully controlled, 'like two people who've only just met. No recriminations over the past, just live for the present. Do you think you could manage that?'

The strangely tentative note in his voice gave Laurel the confidence to meet his eyes at last. They were like deep rock pools, dark and unfathomable, but at least they were no longer filled with the bitter contempt she had seen in them so often before. She felt herself relax slightly. His offer of a truce seemed like a lifeline thrown to a drowning swimmer. If they were to live only for the present, with no reference to the past, then surely she could continue to play her part as Lorraine? She *had* to, for Jenny's sake, she reminded herself as her conscience gave a painful twist.

'I think I could,' she said hesitantly, then, seeing the way his face relaxed, she found her courage growing and smiled tremulously, her green eyes lighting softly. 'Yes, I could—I'd like that.'

Laurel's smile had a dramatic effect on Hal. He drew in his breath, his eyes darkening suddenly. Slowly he reached out a hand and traced the delicate line of her cheekbone with infinite care as if he was afraid the fragile bones might break under his touch. Then his fingers slid upwards, into her hair, closing around the silky strands.

'You're very beautiful, Lori,' he said huskily. 'I've only got to look at you to want you. Maybe it's not enough to build a marriage on, but it should get us through the next two months.'

There it was again, that uneven, almost regretful edge to his voice that was painfully destructive to Laurel's conviction that what she was doing was right, the only way open to her of helping Jenny, so that for the second time that evening she almost weakened and told him everything. But Hal's final words, with their reminder of the way he was prepared to use his wife, as he believed her to be, for his own selfish ends hardened her resolve and, forcing herself to ignore the appealing tone of his voice, she adopted an air of careless insouciance that stunned her by succeeding better than she had ever expected.

'Didn't you say something about a meal? I'm starving!'

Her mind flinched away from the memory of the way Hal's face had hardened at her words as she dragged herself back to the present, embarrassingly aware of the way she had remained absorbed in her thoughts, to Jan Tillotson's evident confusion.

'Where's—Hal?' she asked awkwardly, his name sounding strange and alien on her tongue.

'In his study.' The housekeeper laughed. 'When he's in there I always leave him alone. It's more than my life's worth to disturb him! I usually take coffee in once or twice, but I get in and out as quickly as possible.'

'Dangerous, is he?' Laurel's tone was abstracted. Jan's words had brought her up sharp against the fact of how little she actually knew about this man whose wife she was pretending to be. Once more her thoughts went back to the previous night when, after the meal was over, Hal had abruptly got to his feet with a curt, 'Well, I'll say goodnight.'

'Are you going to bed?' Laurel questioned, her confusion increasing as he shook his dark head.

'I'm going to do some work.' Dark eyes mocked her wickedly. 'I have to do something to take my mind off that seductive little body of yours. Sleep well.'

And surprisingly Laurel had slept easily and deeply, waking to find herself as alone in the double bed as she had been when she had got into it the night before. Only the imprint of another person's head on the other pillow had given any indication that Hal had slept there at all. He must have come to bed very late, when she was soundly asleep, she had decided, colour washing her cheeks at the thought, and was up before she even stirred.

She had no idea what sort of work had occupied him late into the night and again this morning, but there was no way she could ask Jan about it. Whatever explanation Hal had given her, it must have included the fact that she was his wife, and it would look strange to say the least if she didn't know what her supposed husband's job was.

'What are your plans for the day?' the housekeeper was asking. 'It's a beautiful morning, why don't you go down on to the beach for a while?'

'Oh, but wouldn't you like me to help you?' Laurel put in hastily. The idea of some time alone on the beach was strongly appealing, but she wasn't here to enjoy herself and she would feel better if she could do something that would make her feel that she was earning the money Hal had paid her.

Jan Tillotson shook her head firmly. 'I've got everything in hand here and you look as if you could do with some sun on your face—off you go!'

Laurel had collected her jacket and was crossing the hall on her way to the front door when a cool voice behind her brought her swinging round.

'Where do you think you're going?' demanded Hal. Silent as a cat, he had come out of his study and was standing, very tall and darkly disturbing, at the foot of the stairs.

'For a walk.' Laurel's tone was defensive in response to the accusing note in his voice. 'Along the cliff and on to the beach—with your permission, of course,' she added sarcastically, the all too familiar prickly feeling taking hold of her in spite of her attempts to suppress it.

'You're not a prisoner, Lori,' Hal returned mildly. 'Why don't you take Jet? He needs the exercise.'

Laurel's hard-won control of her expression weakened at this careless fulfilment of her childhood dream and a smile softened her tautly guarded face. 'Could I?'

The swift change in Hal's expression told her that her reaction had been unexpected, that it had stunned him, but in the same moment cold realism gave her a less pleasant explanation for Hal's offer and immediately the delight faded from her eyes.

'Is Jet to be a guard dog?' she demanded, hiding a sudden and disconcertingly sharp stab of disappointment behind a cold façade. 'Wouldn't you like to come yourself to make sure I don't escape?'

'I have work to do.' Hal's tone was coldly dismissive; was this how he had reacted when Lorraine had protested at his neglect of her? 'As I said, you're not a prisoner. Take care on the path down to the beach, it's pretty steep.'

He turned and went back into his study, apparently putting all thought of her out of his mind with an ease that was positively insulting.

'Well!' Laurel exclaimed in exasperation, directed as much at herself as at Hal as she realised that his indifference had piqued her more than she cared to admit. This must be how Lorraine had felt, she thought, wincing at the stab of pain that accompanied any memory of her twin. If Hal had treated her in this way, it was no wonder she had found herself unable to tolerate his neglect.

But once outside, with Jet bounding ahead of her, Laurel forgot such unhappy thoughts as she lifted her face to the sun, tossing back her hair and taking deep exhilarating breaths of the sea-tanged air, feeling her senses come gloriously alive. It was a long, long time since she had been completely free in this way, and the feeling intoxicated her as she scrambled down the path to the beach, pulling off her shoes to run across the expanse of sand, Jet jumping and barking beside her. All the tension and stress of the past few days dropped from her as she sped along, her hair flowing out behind her like a silken red-gold banner. It was as if time had somehow slipped and she was the Laurel of years before, on that untypical family holiday, able, for a few moments at least, to throw off the anxieties and responsibilities that were her constant companions every hour of the day. She ran until her breath gave out, finally collapsing in a breathless heap, Jet flopping down at her feet, his tongue lolling, his eyes alert, ready to go again as soon as she moved.

'You crazy creature!' Laughing, she hugged him to her, burying her face in the sleek darkness of his fur. 'I wish you were mine! Jenny would love——'

She broke off abruptly as she heard what she had said. *Jenny!* She had actually forgotten about her sister. Her euphoric mood evaporated swiftly, reality returning as if a cloud had suddenly covered the sun, and, gazing round at the soft golden sand, the sea shining clear blue, she pictured in her mind her small sister's first visit to the seaside. In the beginning Jenny had been overawed by the wide expanse of the shore, the movement of the waves, but then she had gained confidence and had chased in and out of the sea for hours, laughing gaily as the white foam broke over her feet until finally she had spun round and round on the sand, dancing for pure joy.

Remembering that moment, anguished tears clouded Laurel's eyes and her heart ached deep inside her. Jenny *had* to get better; that was all that mattered. Nothing she could do would bring Lorraine back, but at least she could ensure that her younger sister had a future to look forward to. That thought reminded her of Hal and the impossible bargain she had made with him. He had given her a reprieve, but for how long? Could she really hope to hold him off for all of the two months ahead of her?

Slowly and reluctantly she got to her feet, heading back the way she had come, her steps dragging as she felt the burden of the situation in which she was trapped descend to enclose her once more. Once, when she glanced up towards the house, she thought she saw a tall, dark figure silhouetted against the sky, watching her. But the brightness of the sun made her eyes water, she had to blink hard to clear them, and when she looked again Hal—if that was who it had been—had gone again.

Jan Tillotson was putting on her coat when Laurel entered the kitchen.

'I'm glad you got back before I left,' she said with a welcoming smile. 'I've left your lunch ready. Mr Rochester usually has his on a tray in the study. About dinner——'

'Oh, don't worry, I'll see to that,' Laurel assured her, struggling to hide the unease she felt at the prospect of the housekeeper's departure. She had hoped to have Jan's company as a buffer against Hal's abrasive personality for a few hours yet.

'Well, I made a cheesecake—it's in the fridge—and there's plenty of stuff in the freezer. I'll be back tomorrow. I only work mornings except when Mr Rochester has guests coming—I come in at the weekends then. Oh, Mr Rochester asked me to tell you not to disturb him—for any reason, he said—you know what he's like.'

'Mmm,' Laurel murmured vaguely. She didn't know, but she was certainly beginning to guess. How Lorraine, who loved a full social life and plenty of people round her, must have hated the isolation Hal imposed on her if his behaviour today was typical of their marriage! Locked in her own unhappy thoughts, she barely heard Jan's cheerful farewell, only coming back to the present when she heard the housekeeper's car drive away and realised that she was alone again.

The silence in the house seemed oppressive without Jan's cheerful presence. It was just twelve o'clock, too early to take Hal's lunch in to him, she told herself, knowing, deep down, that that was just an excuse to avoid confronting him before she absolutely had to. But what was she to do with herself in the meantime? She wasn't used to being at a loss for something to do, working in the shop and caring for Jenny rarely left her any free time. Glancing round the kitchen, she noticed a pile of washing, carefully folded ready for ironing, and her spirits lifted slightly. Here was something she could do; a constructive contribution she could make. It would hardly be worth the money Hal was paying her, but if she could be useful in any small way she would feel so much better and, in the past, during the dark days after her parents' deaths, such small practical tasks had been her salvation: the many jobs involved in caring for a young toddler had given her no time to think, to become overwhelmed by her own personal sorrow.

She was on the last shirt when the kitchen door opened. As Laurel glanced up from her work she saw Hal come to a sudden halt, his eyes narrowing swiftly as they fastened on her face. His expression was unexpected and somehow familiar, but she barely had time to register the fact that it was the same as the one that had been on his face when she had expressed her delight at his suggestion that she take Jet with her earlier, a mixture of surprise and scepticism, before Hal spoke.

'I pay Jan to do that,' he said, an inexplicable note roughening his voice.

'I know.' Laurel's hands were busy as she spoke, neatly folding the freshly ironed shirt, and she found it easier to keep her eyes on what she was doing than to face the probing force of his gaze. 'But she didn't have time to do it before she left and I had nothing——' Her voice trailed off as she glanced up and saw his frown. 'I wanted to do *something*,' she added unevenly. 'You've given me all that money, I want to earn it.'

Just for a second something flickered in those blue eyes, but then it was swept away by a look of openly sexual mockery.

'I can think of a way I'd prefer you to earn it,' he murmured silkily, destroying her hard-won composure at a stroke. Fiery colour flamed in Laurel's cheeks and her fingers tightened on the shirt, crumpling its fresh smoothness. 'But right now I'll settle for lunch—I'm ravenous!'

The rush of relief was so strong that, unthinkingly, Laurel lifted her head to smile straight into his eyes so that she saw him blink hard as if in confusion.

'It's all ready. Why don't you go and sit down and I'll bring it through.'

'You said you had guests coming over the weekend,' Laurel said a short time later in an effort to make conversation over a meal that so far had been conducted in a difficult and oppressive silence. 'How many people are you expecting?'

'Two, maybe three. Adele and Simon are definite— you don't know them, they were never in London when you were around—and Max said he'd come if he could get away.'

Laurel was painfully aware of the change in Hal's tone, the way he was watching her as if waiting for some response. Carefully and quite unnecessarily she straightened the cutlery on her discarded plate, trying to assimilate what he had said. It was a relief to know that she wasn't supposed to recognise the Adele and Simon Hal had spoken of, but the lack of any such comment about Max could only mean that Lorraine would have known his name. She was afraid to make any comment in case she reacted in quite the wrong way. It was safer, she decided, to sidestep the whole issue.

'Adele and Simon who?' she questioned casually, noting with a sinking heart the way Hal's eyebrows drew together in a frown that clearly indicated he knew exactly what she had done.

'Lorrimer,' he said curtly, the frown lightening very slightly as her eyes went to his face in surprise.

'*The* Adele Lorrimer?'

'There's only one that I know of,' Hal stated coolly.

How did Hal know Adele Lorrimer? Once again Laurel was brought up hard against just how little she knew about this man she had adopted as her husband. Adele Lorrimer was the new name in the film world, an actress whose talent and dark, striking beauty made her the hottest property around. Her latest film, *Chase the Dawn*, was considered to be a potential Oscar winner, and it was breaking all box-office records wherever it was shown. Only last month Laurel and Barbara had bullied the latter's husband into babysitting for Jenny and Barbara's three children and had taken themselves off to town to see it. They had sat entranced throughout the film, and Laurel felt that some of the scenes from it would live in her mind forever. She was longing to ask Hal how they had met, but knew she couldn't take the risk, it might be something Lorraine would have known only too well.

'Why does that bother you, Lori?' asked Hal, misinterpreting her silence. 'Not jealous, are you? You weren't in my life at the time—to the best of my knowledge you'd gone out of it for ever—so why should it upset you?'

'Jealous?' Laurel's voice was brittle. 'Why should I be jealous?' But even as she spoke the words a picture of Adele Lorrimer came into her mind and she found that the thought of Hal with the raven-haired beauty had a disturbing effect on her equanimity. Hastily she got to her feet. 'I'll take the plates through into the kitchen. Do you want coffee?'

Hal shook his head. 'Not for me, thanks, I have to get back to work.'

When Laurel simply nodded he glanced at her sharply as if he had expected some other reaction, but a moment later he got up out of his chair and left the room without another word.

Left alone, Laurel cleared the plates away and washed up, then wandered back into the big living-room, unsure of what to do for the rest of the day. She didn't dare invade the sanctum of Hal's study to find out if there was anything practical she could do, she had had strict instructions to stay away, and the implications of those instructions were as clear as if a physical barrier had been erected between herself and Hal. Whatever occupied him in his study was an aspect of his life in which she had no part—in which *Lorraine* had no part, she reminded herself hastily, shocked to find that she had taken his attitude personally when in fact it was no such thing.

Once again the memory of her twin's complaint that Hal had neglected her surfaced in her mind, and an ache of distress tugged at her thoughts as she acknowledged how much Lorraine would have hated being left to her own devices like this. Well, she wasn't her twin; she was used to being on her own—there had been so many nights when Jenny was in bed and she had had to be content with her own company and she had managed then—but somehow today it seemed so much harder.

She was missing Jenny, Laurel decided, experiencing a rush of longing, intense as a physical pain, to talk to her young sister. But the telephone was in the hall, just outside the door to Hal's study, and she had promised the ward sister she would only ring during evening visiting time to ensure that her calls didn't clash with doctors' rounds or some other event. She would have to contain herself until six o'clock—but in the meantime she needed something to distract her from this unsettled, restless feeling. A glance at the overflowing bookshelves gave her inspiration.

The array of books on the shelves was almost overwhelming. The problem was not to find a book that would interest her but which one of many she wanted to read she would actually choose. She spent several minutes just browsing, dipping into a volume here and there, then suddenly a title caught her eye and shock made her stare at it blankly, her brain not making the logical connection—*Chase the Dawn* by H. E. Rochester.

Very slowly Laurel's hand reached out and took the book from the shelf. Memories flooded her mind: herself and Barbara discussing the film: Barbara saying, 'How could any man get into the mind of a woman like that? I'd love to read the book!'; her own enthusiastic agreement and their joint consternation when they realised that, having arrived a few minutes late, when the film had started, they had missed the name of the author. They had promised themselves that they would find out, in fact Laurel had been planning a trip to the library to do just that on the day Lorraine had arrived back in her life, and after that any such thought had been swept from her mind.

H. E. Rochester—Hal Rochester! *Hal* had written the novel and the screenplay of the film that had taken Laurel into a world in which she had become so totally absorbed that the return to reality had come as a distinct shock. And now she had no need to wonder how Hal had come to know Adele Lorrimer; obviously he must have met her when he was working on the film.

Once again that disturbing sense of disquietude at the thought of Hal and the beautiful actress rocked her mental balance, and in an effort to distract herself Laurel studied the other books on the same shelf, noting several other titles with Hal's name on the spine, two of which she vaguely recalled had won literary awards and one of them had also been made into a film. Her heart quickened pace with excitement. Hal's isolation in his study was now perfectly explicable; he must be writing. Her head spun at the thought that the man she was living with was the exceptionally talented writer whose fine mind had created *Chase the Dawn*, the film that had had so much critical acclaim showered on it in recent months.

But how could *Lorraine* have met him? Remembering her twin's impatience with anything literary, her unwillingness to read anything beyond the latest issue of a fashion magazine, unlike Laurel who loved her literature lessons at school and read almost anything she could lay her hands on, she found it impossible to imagine how her sister and Hal had ever found any point of contact. But then, of course, she recalled bitterly, she was forgetting the overwhelming force of the physical attraction Hal had openly admitted to. But that alone wasn't enough to keep them together, a marriage needed much more, so had Lorraine's marriage been doomed from the start, even before Hal had neglected her in favour of his work? When the suspicion that perhaps Hal had shut himself away so much because her twin had taken no interest in his work slid into her mind Laurel shivered as a sensation like tiny, icy footprints crept down her spine.

Slowly she moved over to a chair and sank down on it, opening the copy of Hal's novel as she did so. From the first page she was lost to the world, absorbed in the power of the book as she had been in the film, oblivious to the passage of time as she read on and on. It wasn't until a feeling in the pit of her stomach that she realised with a shock was one of hunger roused her that she thought to look at the clock. A wave of near panic swept over her as she saw that it was well after six.

Jenny! The thought brought her to her feet in a rush, ignoring the protests of muscles cramped from being too long in one position. The little girl would be waiting to talk to her—but Hal was still in his study. Uncertainly she made her way into the hall, her heart lifting as from behind the closed door of Hal's study she heard the unmistakable clatter of a typewriter. Its noise and the thickness of the door between them would surely be enough to prevent him hearing what she was saying. Snatching at her opportunity, Laurel dialled the number of the hospital in Ashingby.

In the end she needn't have worried what Hal might overhear. The staff nurse was apologetic but firm; she could not let Laurel speak to her sister now, the doctor was with her, he was examining her in order to tell the American specialist how soon she would be able to travel—it was quite possible it would be earlier than they had hoped. Yes, she would tell Jenny that Laurel had phoned. Perhaps if she rang again tomorrow...

Laurel replaced the receiver slowly. It was actually happening! She had never expected that things would move quite so quickly. Money could move mountains, it appeared. It seemed impossible that only days ago she had been in despair, without a hope of helping Jenny, and now——

Her disappointment at not being able to speak to her sister fled as a bubble of joy rose up inside her. Jenny was going to get well, she just *knew* it! Deep down, she was convinced that the operation would be successful. She had only to wait a little while and all her troubles would be over——

A sudden silence from the room beyond the closed door brought her back to reality with a rush. *All* her troubles? The bubble of joy burst suddenly, releasing a stream of cold water over her happiness with the recollection of just how the miracle of the vital operation had been brought about. Hastily Laurel fled back to the living-room, fearful that Hal might come out of his study and knowing she could not face him until she had a stronger grip on her feelings. That brief moment of joy had brought home to her just how important her bargain with Hal was. It would be doubly cruel to destroy Jenny's hopes now when the chance of a cure had become a reality. But the time between now and the day when she could put all this behind her seemed to stretch ahead endlessly. Already she missed Jenny desperately, and if she felt like this now, after only three days, how was she going to cope with the two *months* Hal had insisted on? And when those two months were up, a worrying little voice inside her head murmured, would she really ever be able to put it completely behind her, or would the memory of the deceit she had practised linger to haunt her for the rest of her life?

With an effort she pushed such disturbing thoughts to the back of her mind and turned as always to practical matters to divert her. If she was hungry then Hal must be too, and she set about preparations for a meal, feeling herself relax as she turned to something she could handle without any doubts. The sun still shone brightly outside, and she left the kitchen door open so that its light spilled into the room.

At first she couldn't tell where the noise came from. Soft and low, it was like the whine of an animal in pain, making her turn towards the door. A cry of shock escaped her as she saw Jet stumbling towards her on three legs, the fourth held awkwardly off the ground. As he came nearer Laurel saw the ugly gash on his front paw.

'Oh, Jet! Come here, boy.' Crouching down, Laurel held out a hand to the animal, who limped closer, making a feeble attempt to wag his tail. 'What have you done to yourself?'

A quick examination of the injury showed that it was not deep but long and thin and painful-looking. Jet must have caught himself on some barbed wire or something similar. The cut would need bathing and bandaging. Abandoning the meal half made, Laurel hurried upstairs to the bathroom where she'd seen a first aid box to collect antiseptic, cotton wool and a bandage and, soothing Jet with soft, quiet words, set about dealing with his injury.

She was just winding the bandage around the dog's paw when the door behind her opened. She had no need to wonder who had come in, even if they hadn't been alone in the house, the instinctive, prickling awareness that ran down her spine would have told her it was Hal. What she wasn't prepared for when she turned her head to look at him was his abrupt loss of colour, the look of shocked concern that flashed across his face and the shaken note in his voice when he spoke.

'What the hell's happened? Lori?'

'It's all right, it's not me that's hurt.' Laurel stumbled over the words. The expression on Hal's face was having the most disturbing effect on her heart, making it seem to be beating high up in her throat. 'Jet cut his leg—I was just cleaning it——'

She moved so that Hal could see the dog, previously hidden by her body. Jet's tail thumped the floor at the sight of his master, but Hal spared him only the briefest glance before his eyes went back to Laurel.

'*You* cleaned it?'

'Well, you were working and I didn't want to disturb you.'

Hal moved to crouch down beside the dog, his strong hands gently picking up the injured paw as he examined Laurel's handiwork.

'You've made a good job of this.' An echo of his initial shock still roughened his voice.

'I just did what I thought best. Will he be all right, or should we get him to a vet?'

Hal shook his dark head. 'He'll be fine in a day or so—won't you, boy?'

Watching as he stroked the dog's sleek head, Laurel felt a stunning flash of envy sear through her as she saw the softening of his face, the smile that changed it from the hard, distant mask she saw so often. Her thoughts flew to the memory of how it had felt to have those powerful but gentle hands touch her body—— She dragged her thoughts back from the dangerous path they were taking as Hal straightened up and glanced around.

'We'd better get this mess cleared up.'

Only then did Laurel become aware of the scene that had met his eyes when he had first come into the room— the spots of blood on the floor, the reddened water in a bowl, the stained cotton wool—and now, belatedly, she realised just what had put that note of stunned disbelief in his voice.

Lorraine had never been able to stand the sight of blood. Even the slightest cut on her hand had been enough to send her into hysterics; she would never have been able to cope with Jet's injury. But Laurel had spent five years caring for an active, boisterous sister who always seemed to be in some scrape or other. She had lost count of the number of grazed knees or cut fingers she had had to deal with. In her concern for Jet's welfare she had never stopped to consider that she might be acting out of character for Lorraine, but now she quailed inside at the thought of what she might have revealed inadvertently.

But Hal appeared to have forgotten, or at least to be ignoring, his 'wife's' uncharacteristic behaviour.

'I'm grateful to you for taking care of Jet so promptly. I'm afraid I get lost to the world when I'm working——'

Dimly Laurel caught the note of self-reproach in Hal's voice. Would she be a fool to hope that some of that reproach came from guilt at having left *her* alone too? Pain stabbed at her with the thought that, if so, such a realisation had come far too late to help Lorraine. From a dark, hidden corner of her mind came a picture of her twin's white, still face and she had to bite down hard on her lower lip to hold back the cry of anguish that almost escaped her as all colour fled from her cheeks.

'Lori?' Hal's voice was sharp with concern. 'Are you all right?'

With a gigantic effort Laurel forced a faint smile and spoke in what she hoped was a calmly practical voice. 'I'll clean the floor if you'll deal with the rest. We'll soon have things sorted out.'

This was how she'd always coped before, burying her pain in the practical when she had longed for a shoulder to cry on, a pair of strong arms to hold her, but somehow it didn't serve her as well this time. The urge to turn to Hal, fling herself into his arms and sob out the whole story was almost overwhelming, but the knowledge that such an action would mean admitting to the whole truth held her back. Think of Jenny, she told herself fiercely, ruthlessly forcing back the tears that burned in her eyes and keeping her head bent so that the coppery fall of her hair hid her face as she directed her feelings into actions, cleaning the floor with a concentrated determination until she felt brave enough to face Hal again.

'I'd better finish making dinner,' she said when the kitchen had been restored to its former spotless state. 'It's almost ready.'

She picked up the knife with which she had been peeling potatoes, but her hand shook so much that she had to put it down again. Firm fingers closed over her arms, turning her towards the door.

'I'll do that,' Hal said quietly. 'You've done enough. You look washed out.'

'But I——' Laurel's protest was feeble. The stress of the last few days had caught up with her, the pain of her memories and the weak longing to be in Hal's arms had shaken her more than she dared admit. She felt drained and exhausted, unable to resist as he pushed her towards the living-room.

'Go and relax. I'll manage in here.'

Perhaps he would consider her numbed behaviour as a belated reaction to the sight of blood, Laurel thought hazily as she curled up on the settee. She had come dangerously close to giving herself away. The trouble was she wasn't a very good liar; she had always prided herself on being scrupulously honest, and it went against all the laws by which she lived her life to deceive anyone, even the cold, callous husband Lorraine had described.

But was Hal really all that her twin had made him out to be? Blurred by tiredness, the image of his face in the moment he had come into the kitchen—when he had thought that *she* was the one who was hurt—floated in her mind. She hadn't imagined the shocked concern on his face, just as she couldn't deceive herself that his consideration just now was the behaviour of a man who cared nothing for his wife. She knew she should try to think, to work out the implications of his actions with regard to her position, but a tidal wave of weariness swamped her and with a sigh she leaned back and closed her eyes.

A gentle touch on her arm stirred her, her eyes coming half open to meet Hal's sea-coloured gaze. Struggling up through clouds of sleep, she was unable to resist his arms as they came round her, though she struggled feebly for a moment.

'Hush, my lovely,' soothed Hal, his grip tightening round her. He dropped a light kiss on her forehead as he gathered her close. His arms felt as strong as steel bands around her, imprisoning her against the hardness of his chest.

Not like this! Laurel thought weakly. Not when she wasn't even fully aware of what was happening! But she was too exhausted to fight, a drowsy languor filling her as she lay submissively in Hal's grasp, her eyes closing irresistibly, too heavy to keep open.

'You're worn out.' Was it just the mist that filled her mind, or was Hal's tone really so soft it was like a physical caress? 'Let's have you upstairs.'

Laurel was only vaguely aware of him moving out into the hall and up the stairs, but she roused herself slightly when the warmth of his body left her as he laid her on the bed.

Wake up! she told herself fiercely. Wake up before it's too late! But the exhaustion was too all-pervading to resist and she was incapable of doing more than lift her eyelids very slightly—only to close them again swiftly when she saw how near Hal's face was to her own.

'Hal, no,' she sighed, her voice no more than a whisper. But he caught her words, and she heard his mellow laughter.

'One day, lady, you're going to use my name in a way I like much better.'

She hadn't felt his hands on the buttons of her shirt, unfastening them, so it came as a shock when he eased it from her shoulders and, still with her eyes shut, she tried to curl into a small, defensive ball.

'Lori!' Hal reproved tolerantly, uncoiling her with careful hands. 'You don't make things easy for me!'

She didn't want to make things easy for him, she wanted to fight him with all the strength she had—but that was the trouble, every trace of strength had drained from her and she could only lie limply as Hal dealt as efficiently with her jeans and underwear as he had done with her shirt until, in a very short time and without quite being aware of how she had got there, she was in bed, the sheets cool and soft against her skin. Sleep was clouding her mind again in spite of her struggles against it, but she knew there was something she had to say before it was too late. She couldn't pretend with Hal, not now when her exhaustion had weakened her defences.

'Hal,' she murmured, her voice slurred with tiredness. 'Something to tell you . . .'

Blindly she reached out a hand to where she thought he was and felt warm, strong fingers close around her own in a warm, comforting grasp.

'Not now, my lovely.' Hal's voice seemed to come from a long way away.

Laurel felt the bed give as he slid on to it beside her; gentle fingers stroked her hair back from her face and she thought she felt his lips brush her cheek, then, unbelievably, he was easing away, moving off the bed. Already drifting away on a deep sea of sleep, Laurel scarcely registered the click of the door behind him as he left the room.

CHAPTER SIX

THE BRIGHT sun of the past few days had been replaced by a thick sea mist that hung heavily and damply around the house, obscuring everything other than a few hazy outlines of trees and shrubs and making the cliff edge completely invisible. There was a distinct chill in the air too, so that Laurel was glad of the extra warmth of the white cotton sweater, one of the ones Hal had bought for her, which she wore with a bright yellow skirt. Because of the weather they hadn't been able to go out this morning, and she couldn't decide whether she felt relieved or sorry that Hal had once more locked himself away in his study, the sound of his typewriter the only evidence of his existence.

Hal. Her thoughts went back over the three days since Jet had cut his paw; three days that had been a disturbing mixture of pleasure and deep uncertainty which had at times bordered on black despair.

Her mind had been in turmoil since the moment she had woken, torn by the conflict between the memory of the way Lorraine had described her husband and the evidence of his actions the night before. He had been considerate, gentle. He had undressed her, put her to bed, and she had been weak, totally defenceless, and yet he hadn't touched her. The thought made her tremble because it was so completely incomprehensible. Hal had made his physical desire for her so plain that it seemed impossible that he should not have taken advantage of the fact that she was unable to resist him. His restraint was totally at odds with the man she had believed him to be, and that fact forced her to reconsider all the assumptions she had made about Hal from the moment she had first met him and even before when, with Lorraine's distress uppermost in her mind, she had labelled Hal Rochester as a callous, uncaring monster without even having seen him.

Such thoughts left her feeling rawly vulnerable, so that she was ill prepared for the moment when, going downstairs, she found that, instead of being shut away in his study as she had anticipated, Hal was in the living-room, lingering over a cup of coffee and obviously not intending to work that morning. The sight of his powerful body casually dressed in a cream-coloured short-sleeved shirt and toning cotton trousers rocked her already precarious equanimity, forcing her to remember how it had felt to be held close in those muscular arms, her head resting against the hard strength of his shoulder, the memory all the more disconcerting because she knew that she should have felt afraid, been fearful of Hal and his intentions, but she hadn't. Instead she had felt safe, secure and protected, and the confusion that thought brought meant that she barely heard Hal's greeting and had to focus her mind swiftly to catch his next words.

'Where would you like to go today?'

'Like to go?' Laurel echoed faintly, unsure that she had heard him aright, her confusion increasing at his smiling nod.

'It's a glorious day, far too nice to waste stuck inside. I thought we could go out for the day.'

I thought *we* could go out—Hal's words echoed hollowly inside Laurel's head. His unexpected invitation had thrown her off balance mentally, his casual 'we' implying a sharing that at another time, in other circumstances, she might have welcomed with delight but that here and now twisted her nerves into tight, painful knots.

'But what about your work? I don't want to keep you away from it.'

Hal's shrug dismissed his writing with a carelessness that severely threatened her precarious hold on her composure as it further undermined her picture of him as a man whose selfish neglect had led to Lorraine's unhappiness.

'My work can wait,' he said easily, then, seeing the doubt that still clouded her face, added, 'All right, we'll compromise. I'll spend the mornings with you and work in the afternoons—does that suit you?'

Laurel was only able to nod a silent agreement, too shaken by this very different side of Hal and the way it threatened her conviction that he deserved everything he got to be able to force her tongue to frame a single word.

'I thought we'd go out along the Brigg,' he continued, showing no sign either by word or change of expression of being aware of her mental conflict, though she doubted that that keen blue gaze could have missed the way her colour came and went, the uncertainty that clouded the clear, bright green of her eyes. Remembering his suggestion that they should treat each other as if they had only just met, she could only put his silence down to a tactful avoidance of any possible cause of argument, a determination to keep the peace at all costs that was somehow infinitely more disturbing than the angry hostility or bitter sarcasm she had come to expect from him. 'The tide's way out this morning, so we'd be able to walk right to the Point.' He hesitated unexpectedly and Laurel was startled to see that the glance he shot her was touched with a hint of uncertainty. 'Or if you'd prefer to go to Marborough—go round the shops——?'

'Oh, no.'

Through the haze that clouded her mind, one thing was clear. She had never liked wandering round the shops just for the sake of it, and after the experience of buying the new clothes Hal had insisted on she had seen as much of the town as she wanted to for quite some time. Besides, the Brigg, the huge stretch of rock that curved out into the bay, had fascinated her from the moment she had first seen it.

'I'd love to explore the Brigg. Alec Tracey said you can often find fossils out there.'

It was only later, when they were in the car and heading towards Nunham, that Laurel realised why Hal had offered the alternative suggestion. Given such a choice, Lorraine wouldn't have hesitated, Marborough and its shops would have won hands down over the prospect of scrambling over the rocky path that led to Nunham Point. For a moment she considered telling Hal that she had changed her mind. That, she thought with a mixture of anguish and wryness, was just the sort of thing he might expect from his wife; Lorraine had always been inconsistent, to say the least. But then the car rounded a bend in the road and ahead of her she saw the wide sweep of the bay and the Brigg, rising, starkly magnificent, out of the sun-speckled sea, and the idea fled before a wave of longing to be herself just this once. She didn't care if it might be wiser, safer, to choose the sort of outing Lorraine would have preferred. She *wanted* to explore the Brigg.

'Coffee's ready.' Jan Tillotson's voice broke into Laurel's thoughts, making her realise that she had been staring unseeingly out of the kitchen window for who knew how long. 'We can put our feet up for a while now. Everything's just about done. I really appreciate you helping me like this—you didn't have to do it.'

'I enjoyed it.'

Laurel hoped her smile hid the way she really felt, because the truth was that her attempt to lose herself in hard, practical work by helping Jan with the cleaning had failed to provide the distraction she needed. Her hands had been busy, but the lack of concentration needed for the routine tasks had given her too much time to think—and thinking led nowhere; she just ended up going round and round in circles.

She had found the trip to the Brigg far more enjoyable than she had ever anticipated. Hal seemed to have thrown off the hostile, aggressive mood she had come to dread and proved himself stimulating and fascinating company. He had a fund of knowledge of the history of the area and was able to recount tales of the many ships that had foundered against the jagged rocks around the coast. He had taken her hand quite naturally, almost unconsciously, to help her over the more difficult parts of their walk when the rocks were damp and treacherously slimy with seaweed, and he had shown infinite patience with her childlike determination to find at least one of the fossils that the hotel landlord had assured Laurel littered the rocky shore, sharing her delight when at last she came across a small, rather battered ammonite and held it aloft in triumph.

'Happy now?' Hal enquired, laughter warming his eyes so that they looked like the sea in the bay, glinting in the sun.

'Yes, quite happy.'

Seeing him like this, the cold, hard man she had thought was Hal completely hidden behind this new and much more approachable exterior, Laurel felt her heart turn over and knew a desperate longing to freeze the moment for ever. Unable to meet his eyes with any degree of equanimity, she dropped her gaze to the stone in her hand, tracing the shape of the long-dead animal with fingers that shook perceptibly.

'It's rather awe-inspiring, isn't it—to think that once, thousands of years ago, this was a living creature and now it's part of these rocks. It makes me feel very insignificant.'

'I know.' Hal's voice was low and slightly husky. 'When I come out here I feel it's like going into a time-slip, as if time doesn't exist any more, as if it's suspended.'

Laurel nodded slowly, a quiver running through her at the thought of how close Hal's words had come to her own feelings only moments before. Away from the house like this, with the primitive beauty of the sea and the cliffs around her, she felt as if all her worries, all her doubts had ceased to exist. There was just herself and Hal in this tiny capsule of time.

'My watch tells me we've been here nearly two hours, but these rocks change so little, so slowly, that it could be two days, two weeks——' She broke off abruptly, realising what she had been about to say.

'Two months,' Hal finished for her.

Laurel flinched as his words brought the first intrusion of reality into her private idyll of peace. Seeing Hal's face with the clear light of the sun on it, she felt as if she was seeing it for the very first time. She had thought it a hard, unyielding face without any redeeming trace of gentleness or warmth. Why hadn't she noticed the laughter-lines that feathered out from his eyes, the marks etched beside his mouth that showed how often, in other circumstances, those firm, straight lips had curved into a smile? So when had Hal stopped smiling? Had Lorraine been responsible for the way his expression now fell into the harsh, stern appearance that had so repelled her at their first meeting? Suddenly the two months that had seemed an eternity to her only days before now seemed far too short a time in which to get to know and understand the complex man Hal really was. If only there really was such a thing as a time-slip, so that you could go back—— To her shock and consternation, Laurel found that she had spoken the words out loud.

'And when would you want to go back to, Lori?'

When would she want to go back to? So many times came rushing into Laurel's mind that she found she couldn't think clearly enough to isolate one. Back to the first time she had met him so that she could undo the way she had been cornered into pretending to be Lorraine—to the time before her twin's arrival in Ashingby, before Jenny's accident—oh, if only she could! But then, clear and sharp, with a force that made her head reel, she knew which time she would really choose. If only it were possible to go back to the days before Hal had met Lorraine so that they could really see each other as strangers, without the shadows of the past darkening everything they did or said.

'We could make our own time-slip.' Hal's voice was soft, but his words closed Laurel's throat in panic so that she thought she would never breathe again.

He was reaching out to her, wanting to start again, but it was *Lorraine* he was trying to reach, his *wife*, not the sister who had taken her place. He was offering a chance to forgive and forget, but he didn't know what *she* had done that needed to be forgiven, and if Jenny was to have her chance of a future he must never know. There could be no chance to start again, not for herself and Hal, the way she had deceived him must always come between them. Laurel's hand closed tightly over the hard form of the fossil, the stone digging painfully into her hand as she faced the fact that the only way open to her was to pretend that she hadn't understood.

'But unfortunately we can't. We agreed we'd spend the morning out and you could work in the afternoon. If we don't make a move the afternoon will be half gone before we get back.'

Not daring to look at Hal's face to see the effect her words had had on him, she turned and set off back towards the beach, her progress made difficult by the hot tears that burned in her eyes, blurring her vision.

* * *

'It's a pity the weather's spoilt itself.' Jan Tillotson's voice broke into her thoughts. 'You must miss your trips out.'

Laurel managed a wordless murmur that might have been agreement. After the trip to the Brigg she had expected that Hal would forget about his plan to spend at least part of the day with her, but she had been proved wrong. He had been waiting for her when she got up the next day, and the day after that, and together they had explored the countryside around Nunham, calling in at some small village pub for lunch over which they had lingered so that, as Laurel had predicted that first day, by the time they returned home the time allotted to Hal's work had been eroded by the hours he had spent with her.

Still, Laurel had insisted that once they were home he must work and, as she had anticipated, as soon as he was at his desk he was lost to her, absorbed in the world he was creating, the sound of his typewriter echoing through the silent house late into the night. She could still hear it long after she had gone to bed—alone because, whether from deliberate policy or because his work kept him at his desk, Hal never joined her in the double bed until well after she was asleep and he had always gone in the morning when she awoke.

Remembering the way Hal had said, 'I have to do something to keep my mind off that seductive little body of yours,' Laurel had to admit that his actions were probably deliberate, but the thought of the reprieve from his attentions which had once seemed her only hope of getting through the ordeal of the two months spent with Hal now brought her no comfort at all. Instead it was like another twist to the knife that was her conscience, bringing with it implications of patience and consideration that she had never attributed to Hal before.

'Well, we'd better enjoy our peace while we've got it.' Jan Tillotson appeared oblivious to Laurel's abstracted silence. 'Once Mr Rochester's guests arrive it'll be all go.'

'What are they like?' Laurel asked cautiously, not at all sure whether Jan too would expect her to know about any of the visitors.

'I don't know the Lorrimers—I've never met them— but that Max—well——' The housekeeper's mouth twisted. 'He thinks he's God's gift to women—he'll flirt with anything in a skirt—so you be warned.'

'Oh, I'll be careful,' Laurel assured her, unable to erase the uneven note from her voice as she admitted privately with an uncomfortable twisting of her nerves just how careful she was going to have to be, because the womanising Max was the man she, or rather Lorraine, was supposed to know.

With Jan's departure a heavy silence settled on the house, one that preyed on Laurel's nerves, leaving her torn between an overwhelming sense of loneliness when she contrasted this solitary afternoon with the past three days she had spent with Hal and a strong desire to avoid his company as much as was humanly possible. She had come to enjoy being with him—enjoy it too much for her own safety and mental balance—and she felt it would be impossible to face him without letting her innermost thoughts show.

Who was Hal Rochester really? The contrast between his cold-blooded using of the woman he thought was his wife and the powerful yet sensitive mind revealed in his book seemed impossible to reconcile or explain, and that quandary drove Laurel to pick up the novel again in the hope that she might find some way of resolving the conflict.

As before, the printed words wove their own sort of magic around her and she remained absorbed for hours, breaking off only for the vital phone call to Jenny. The nightly talk with her small sister had come to seem like a lifeline, the brief contact with the little girl for whom she had committed herself to this nightmare in the first place being the only thing that kept her from being swept away in the floodtide of doubt and confusion that assailed her in every waking moment.

As before, the clatter of Hal's typewriter drowned her conversation, a fact for which she was intensely grateful, because Jenny was obviously tired and fractious, fretting at the way she was deprived of Laurel's company, and Laurel had to spend a long time soothing her, reassuring her that all was well, her own voice breaking noticeably as she realised the conflict between her firm, confident words and the truth of how she was really feeling. When, reluctantly, she finally put the receiver down she stood for a moment, her eyes closed, helpless before the wave of desolation that swept through her. She couldn't go on like this. The fragile link of the telephone just wasn't enough. She had to *see* Jenny, give herself tangible evidence of the fact that, in the end, all this really would be worthwhile. But how could she get away? Would Hal——?

The shrill sound of the telephone bell jolted her out of her unhappy reverie, making her snatch her hand away from the receiver as if she had been burned. She heard the sudden silence from the study before Hal lifted the receiver on his extension. Through the door she heard him give his number, his voice crisp and clear, bringing back memories of the time she had tried to ring him from Ashingby and her own irrational panic at realising that she was connected to an answering machine.

Oh, *why* hadn't she spoken to him then! Why hadn't she given him the whole story, explained that she was Lorraine's sister and so saved herself from the horror of that first meeting when he had been so convinced that she was her twin? But if she had, would he have believed her? With a dull ache in her heart Laurel remembered that Lorraine had told Hal that she had no family alive, and the ache sharpened to a stabbing pain as she was forced to admit that the thoughtless selfishness of that was nothing new.

'Max? What do you want?'

Hal's voice from behind the study door penetrated the clouds of unhappiness that filled Laurel's mind and with a shock she registered the curt hostility of his tone. Max was one of the visitors due at Highcliff the day after tomorrow. Hal had already told her that he was driving down to London to collect Adele and Simon first thing in the morning but that Max would make his own way to the house. He was, she had assumed, a friend, someone both Hal and Lorraine had liked—but Hal's tone of voice made a nonsense of that assumption, which left only one possible explanation—that Max was a special friend of *Lorraine's*.

Panic blurred Laurel's thoughts. How could she handle this without giving herself away completely? Oh, if only she could see Jenny! Then she might have the mental strength to go through with it.

A sudden thought struck her, coming so clear and sharp that Hal's conversation faded as she considered it. Hal was going to London. He didn't plan to be back until the following day. There might just be time——
Her heart raced as she hurried back to the living-room to consult the railway timetable she had in her handbag.

She was deep in the intricacies of routes and connections when the door opened and Hal strode into the room, making Laurel start guiltily and hastily push the betraying timetable into the pocket of her skirt. Had Hal noticed her action? Her heart lurched uncomfortably at the thought, her unease increasing a hundredfold when she saw the tautness of the muscles of Hal's face, the look in his eyes that spoke of a return to the coldly distant mood that had been missing for the past three days. Nervously she tried a smile, her spirits sinking when it met with no response. *Had* he seen her hide the timetable, or was his mood perhaps some lingering annoyance after the phone call from Max?

'I'm sorry if I've neglected you.' Laurel was intensely aware of the effort Hal was making to keep his tone even and polite. 'I hope you haven't been too bored.'

'Not at all. I've been reading.'

'Reading?'

The frankly sceptical question made Laurel's heart lurch at the realisation that, in her attempt to smooth over an awkward moment, she had once more stepped out of character as Lorraine. But, after that one moment of near-panic, she found that she didn't care. It mightn't be the wisest or the safest move, but she wanted to talk to Hal about his work, wanted to know more about the mind that had created *Chase the Dawn*.

'Yes, reading.' Defiantly she lifted the book for him to see. Hal's eyes went to the title on the cover, then back to Laurel's face, narrowing swiftly, his dark brows drawing together in a frown.

'What do you think of it?' he said slowly, his voice sounding slightly rough and hoarse as if his throat was dry.

'I love it!' Laurel was unable to tone down her genuine enthusiasm and let it show with a lack of reservation that deepened the frown on Hal's face. 'But then I loved the film too. I can't wait to read your other books.'

She paused, waiting for him to speak, but when he appeared uncharacteristically at a loss for words she hurried on in an attempt to fill the silence.

'What are you working on now? Is it a new novel or another screenplay? I hope that the hours you've been working means it's going well—I tried not to disturb you...'

Her voice faltered under the scrutiny of Hal's intent gaze. Underneath that watchful surface flickered some other, strongly controlled emotion. Laurel prayed it wasn't anger.

'I——' she tried again, but Hal broke in on her abruptly.

'All right, Lori, what's the game?' It wasn't anger that flared in his eyes but something new, something she couldn't interpret.

'I don't know what you mean! I'm not playing any game.'

'No?' Laurel winced at the sarcastic emphasis Hal gave to the single syllable. 'Then why this sudden interest in my writing? You had no interest in it before except as a source of money, so why have you suddenly started reading my books?'

Because I wanted to get to know you, understand you. The words burned on Laurel's tongue, but she was afraid to utter them. Perhaps yesterday she might have done just that, but now the look on Hal's face frightened her. The icy contempt she had seen at their first meeting was back, shrivelling her impulsive words into ashes on her tongue. Something had happened to destroy the tenuous relationship they had begun to build, and she had no idea what it could be. The pain that realisation brought threatened her composure so that she almost retracted her words, declared she wasn't interested after all, but immediately knew she couldn't do it. Lorraine's unhappy words sounded in her head like a reproach, but she had committed herself, she couldn't go back. She wanted to know about the other side of Hal's character, *needed* to know about it, and this might be her only opportunity.

'This isn't any sort of game, Hal,' she told him quietly. 'I——' She hesitated, then decided that the truth was safest. 'I didn't know about your work until I saw the film of *Chase the Dawn*, but after that I knew I just had to read the book. It's a wonderful story, so powerful, and—and I'd like to talk to you about it—please.'

If she had struck him in the face Hal couldn't have looked more stunned. Laurel could see the tautness of the muscles in his jaw, his shoulders and, with the memory of his bitter declaration that Lorraine had taken no interest in his work other than because of the money it brought in ringing inside her head, she couldn't help recalling her own suspicion that perhaps the marriage between this man and her sister had been doomed from the start. Lorraine had said that she'd left her husband because of his neglect, but Laurel was coming to see that the truth was far more complicated than that. She had tried to justify her deception of Hal by telling herself she owed it to Lorraine, that she was only using him as he had used her twin, but now she knew that she also owed it to Hal too to try and find out the truth. What that truth might do to her earlier conviction that what she was doing was the only possible answer, justified by the end to which she was working, Jenny's future, she couldn't bear to think. She only knew it had to be done or she could never live with her conscience.

Hal moved suddenly, coming to sit directly opposite Laurel, resting his elbows on the arms of his chair, his hands clasped, regarding her disturbingly intently over the top of them.

'All right,' he said. 'So talk.'

Laurel wetted her dry lips nervously. She had her chance, he was actually listening to her at last. Dear God, let her not spoil things now!

CHAPTER SEVEN

'WELL, for a start, who was Maria? Because she was a real person, wasn't she—someone you knew?'

The steady gaze of Hal's eyes never wavered for a moment. He seemed to be trying to probe deep down into Laurel's mind, read her innermost thoughts.

'Would you like me to say I based her on you, Lori?' he asked, his tone softly ironical but without that hateful, aggressive quality so many of his taunts had contained before. He seemed to want to provoke her, as someone who has been hurt lashes out at the first person in sight, but the attack was muted and somehow strangely automatic, as if his mind was on other things.

'I wouldn't believe you if you did,' she said carefully, meeting his eyes directly so that she saw the faint glimmer of amusement that lit their darkness. 'So who was she really?'

'My grandmother. That's why the book's set in the Twenties when Gran was a young woman. The life she lived was typical of so many women of that age and yet, in many ways, so very different.' Hal's voice warmed as he spoke and Laurel felt a twist of envy at the thought that his grandmother had known him when he was so much younger, before he had hardened into the man he was now. 'The three husbands are fact too—something of a gift, that!' His laughter was soft, relaxed, and it sent a thrill through Laurel just to hear it.

'And her real love—the man who died. Was that true too?'

Hal nodded slowly. 'Yes. Gran never talked about him much. I had to embroider the details quite a bit to make a story out of it. She only knew him for a week, but she gave him her heart completely. The three men she married never really touched her as he did—she loved him until the day she died.'

Something shivered inside Laurel as Hal spoke, a quivering sense of reaction as if his words had touched a sensitive nerve. A week ago she might not have understood how someone could be so completely knocked off balance, their whole life changed by one brief meeting, but that was before she had met Hal. Suddenly it seemed as if her surroundings, the rain now lashing the windows, had faded into a blur so that she couldn't think, could only feel, every nerve in her body hypersensitive to the sight and sound of Hal so very close to her.

'As a matter of fact, if it hadn't been for that man I wouldn't be here. My father was his child—quite a scandal in those days.'

Laurel could only nod silently. The thought of a world without Hal seemed shocking, empty. In fact she found it hard to believe that she had ever not known him, as if the days before they had met had never existed. She felt hazy and strangely unreal, as if she was on the verge of something very important, a new beginning. This must be how a butterfly feels just before it emerges from the chrysalis, she thought, with a wry, inner smile at the fanciful notion.

'The title came from my grandmother too.' Hal's voice penetrated the mists that clouded her mind. 'She used to have a saying—"Even on the darkest night of your life you can always chase the dawn." She had a great strength of character—an optimism and determination that I wanted to capture.'

'And you did.' Laurel found it hard to speak, her tongue seemed weak as if she hadn't used it for a long time. 'If your grandmother was really like Maria I can see why you admired her so much. I only wish I could have met her. I . . .' Her voice trailed off into an embarrassed silence as she saw the way Hal was looking at her, a faintly ironic twist to his mouth.

'Do you know, Lori,' he said slowly, 'when you're like this I could almost get to like you.'

That hurt, stinging like the flick of a whip, but when she looked into Hal's sea-coloured eyes she saw that the bitter humour hadn't touched them, they were dark and serious, and once more she had the feeling that the satirical taunt had come automatically, almost as a defence mechanism, as if he was unsure of the reaction if he spoke the truth, and that gave her the confidence to push the hurt aside and speak again.

'You're lucky to have known your grandmother so well.' She didn't try to disguise the wistful note that had crept into her voice. 'My father's parents both died before I was born and my mother's didn't live long enough for me to get to know them. There was an uncle—my father's brother—but he emigrated to Australia and Dad lost touch with him. When my parents were killed I wrote to him at the last address we had, but there was no reply. He must have moved away.'

Laurel's voice cracked as she recalled how, in those dark days, she had longed for someone to share her unhappiness with, some member of the family who could offer her the closeness and comfort she gave to Jenny but could not find for herself, especially after Lorraine had left. That particular memory brought such a searing stab of anguish that she launched into speech again to distract herself from her thoughts.

'I'm afraid that was rather typical of my father. He wasn't very good at the ordinary, everyday practicalities of life. He was too busy with his dreams of making a fortune.'

The intensity of Hal's gaze was disturbing. His eyes were so deep and dark that they were almost black, and she felt as if they were mesmerising her, drawing her out of herself, so that when he said quietly, 'Tell me about it,' she found herself doing just that, her voice low but clear as she described her gipsy-like childhood, the constant moves from town to town necessitated by her father's impractical schemes to get rich quick.

'There was a newsagent's, a launderette, even a café, though Dad didn't know the first thing about catering, and all of them failed because of debts he couldn't pay. Occasionally one project would succeed for a time and we would begin to settle, put down roots, but inevitably Dad would lose interest, grow impatient at the slow, steady slog needed to keep the business going and begin to think that the grass was greener on the other side of the fence.'

She had soon come to recognise the signs, the restlessness, the reluctance to leave the house for work in the morning, the avid searching through the newspapers for some other, potentially more profitable scheme, until eventually, with weary resignation, her mother would tell them they were on the move again.

'I don't know how my mother managed. She had to watch every penny she spent and there was never anything left over for luxuries. I remember we went on holiday just once—for a week at Bournemouth. That was the year of the launderette—it did quite well for a time—but then Dad got bored.'

Laurel sighed, staring sightlessly ahead of her, seeing pictures of the past in her mind.

'The thing I remember most about my mother was that she was always sewing—mending clothes or letting them down so that they'd fit. If we needed anything new it had to be a birthday or Christmas present and——'

She broke off abruptly, painfully aware of that betraying 'we'. Would Hal take that to mean just herself and her parents, or would he realise there was more to it than that? Tension twisted her nerves, but Hal's question when it came was so unexpected that for a moment she wasn't sure she had heard right.

'How did you feel about your father?'

'I—I loved him.'

'But weren't you angry? Didn't you ever want to kick out against the way he was ruining your life—and your mother's?'

Lorraine had fought, Laurel remembered, picturing the constant rows her twin had provoked. But then Lorraine had been so much like their father in temperament while Laurel favoured their mother, and Mary Grahame had always been gently resigned, never raising any objections, going along with her husband whatever he did. Which had perhaps been quite the wrong idea, with hindsight Laurel could see that now. And perhaps, following her mother's example, she had done the wrong thing where her twin was concerned too. When Jenny had been born, a surprise addition to the family when the twins were sixteen, the arrival of a baby sister had been, as far as Lorraine was concerned, the last straw, resulting as it did in even greater restrictions on her personal freedom and further financial burdens on the family. She had adamantly refused to have anything to do with the new baby and Laurel had quietly taken over the care of her younger sister, leaving her twin free to do as she pleased. So perhaps, in a way, she had only herself to blame for what had happened later when Lorraine had once more put herself first at Laurel's expense.

'Why did you never tell me this before?' asked Hal and, entangled in a skein of conflicting emotions, Laurel had no control over her tongue.

'Did you ever ask?' she flashed fiercely, no longer knowing if she believed Lorraine's accusations against him or not, only aware that, by his words, he was admitting that, in this area at least, he had been guilty of neglect.

Slowly Hal shook his head, one hand going up to rake through his dark hair in a gesture that betrayed the disturbed state of his thoughts.

'I'm sorry,' he said, his voice rough and uneven.

In the few seconds that followed his apology Laurel experienced a range of complicated feelings that threatened to tear her mind into tiny pieces. An initial swift surge of delight was destroyed by the thought that, for Lorraine, that apology had come too late, but the next moment she felt as if the world was spinning out of her control as she struggled with an emotion that she realised was sheer, blind jealousy at the thought that that apology was meant for her twin and nothing in it was for Laurel herself. Her head felt as if it was going to split apart with the conflict being waged inside it, and hot tears burned in her eyes.

'Lorraine——' Hal began again, but the sound of her twin's name on his lips was too much for Laurel. Scrambling blindly to her feet, she knew only one thing, she had to escape from those searching blue eyes.

'You must be hungry,' she blurted out in a voice that, blurred and thick with emotion, did not sound at all like her own. 'I'll see what Jan's left for us.'

Her flight to the kitchen was awkward and undignified, tears blurring her vision so that she blundered into a chair on the way, but at last she was alone and, with the protection of the closed door between her and Hal, she leaned weakly against the wall and gave in to the tears which would not be held back but cascaded down her cheeks in a torrent that matched the rain which was still falling steadily, drenching the garden, because those tears were not just for her present situation, they were the tears she should have wept years ago but which had never been shed and had stored up in her heart until now, at last, they poured out like a flood-swollen river finally breaking its banks.

She was weeping for her parents whose deaths she had never been able to mourn fully because Jenny had needed her to be strong; for Jenny, small and frail and in pain, so totally dependent on the vital operation to restore her to the healthy, active child she had once been; for Lorraine who had wanted so much out of life and who had found only unhappiness; but most of all she was weeping for herself, because only now did she realise how much her devotion to her family, particularly her sisters, had cost her.

From the moment she had forced herself to identify her twin's body her emotions had been numb, deadened by the shock of what had happened. Even at the funeral she had gone through the simple ceremony with a stoical calm that had amazed and worried Barbara. It was only now that she saw that that numbness had lasted far longer than a few weeks, that the real loss had come five years before when first her parents and then Lorraine had gone out of her life so suddenly. And now, when she was least able to cope with it, the memory of her twin's behaviour just a few days after their parents' deaths which had been sealed away in some private Pandora's box in her mind came back to haunt her.

On the morning after a meeting with the solicitor, a meeting at which it had been revealed just how appalling their father's financial position had been, Laurel had gone to Lorraine's bedroom to waken her sister, only to find her gone. The room was unnaturally bare and tidy, stripped of all Lorraine's possessions, and on the dressing-table lay a note, typical of her twin in its brief flippancy.

'Off to seek my fortune. When I'm rich I'll come back and rescue you. L.'

Laurel had never revealed to anyone, not even Barbara, the sense of betrayal she had felt when she had read that note. Looking back, she now realised how she had buried that feeling, pushing it away as she concentrated on clearing up the mess her father had left behind him and directing all her emotional energies into caring for Jenny. She had taken on that responsibility so willingly, never questioning if it was right, and in much the same way she had accepted her twin's story on the day Lorraine had come to Ashingby, seeking out the sister who had always been there to help when things had gone wrong before.

Just as her mother had always supported her father, no matter how foolish or disturbing his decisions, so too Laurel had been there for Lorraine, to help with her homework, answer a telephone call from a boyfriend to say Lorraine wasn't well when in fact she was preparing to go out with someone else, and when their mother died she had taken on her role too, with Jenny, acting blindly, never putting herself first, never considering her own needs, until her time with Hal had revealed those needs to her with a force that had swept her off balance, carrying her miles away from the path she had thought she was following.

The family loyalty that had blinded her to her father's faults had also blinded her to Lorraine's. Her twin had been desperately unhappy, but Lorraine was very much her father's daughter, so wasn't it possible that she could have been every bit as selfish and mercenary as Hal had accused her of being? And, having admitted that, she now had to reconsider Hal in a new light. His cynicism, his cruelty and cold contempt could all be explained if he had loved Lorraine and she had treated him as carelessly as she had once treated her own sister.

A cold hand curled around her heart, squeezing it mercilessly. If Hal had loved her sister he would be devastated by the deception she had practised on him. He had been treated badly by one member of the family, but what she was doing to him was potentially far worse—if he ever found out. He must *never* find out, she vowed to herself; she could at least spare him that.

But by allowing the friendship that had started to develop between them, she was risking hurting him in a different way. If he thought that at last he and—and *Lorraine*, she forced herself to admit, though it tore her heart in two to do so—were slowly coming to an understanding, then when she left him, apparently for the second time, he would be shattered by this second betrayal. She would have to withdraw from him again, put that vital distance between them, so that in the end all he had lost was a selfish wife and he would never know how different it might have been.

Different because she knew now what had happened to her. She had made the fatal, most terrible mistake of all. She had fallen in love with Hal Rochester, and that love was fated from the start, it had no future. She could never admit to it, because to do so would mean that she would also have to admit that she was not Lorraine—she couldn't love Hal in her sister's name.

So she would have to hold back, however much it hurt. It had to be done for *Hal's* sake, and then when the two months were up she could set him free, leaving him at least his future in which he could find someone else, learn to love again.

When the two months were up—what would she do then? Could she really just take the money and run? But if she didn't Jenny would never know *her* future the way it should be. How could she balance a six-year-old's future against Hal's needs—and her own, a tiny, newly awakened voice inside her head whispered. What of her own needs? Could she ever hope to be happy without Hal? She felt as if she was trapped inside some hugely complicated maze and no matter which twisting, turning path she took she always ended up at the same place, facing the fact that, because of Jenny and Lorraine, there was no future for herself and Hal.

Even to tell Hal the truth would do no good. When he knew how she had deceived him he would hate her, regard her with the same contempt he so clearly felt for Lorraine, and what made things infinitely worse was the fact that she could not deny, even to herself, that his attitude would be justified. She *had* deceived him, burying her true self under a heap of lies. She hated herself for it, so what right had she to hope that he might feel otherwise?

The tears that had poured down her cheeks had stilled, drying in the face of the sheer, blank despair that filled Laurel's mind, when the kitchen door opened. Instinctively Laurel swung away swiftly, hiding her face as she struggled for control.

'Lori?' Hal's voice was soft, questioning. 'What is it?'

'Nothing!' she gasped, unable to control the trembling that shook her as he came to stand at her side, his nearness unbearable when she knew the full extent of the gulf that lay between them. 'Go away!'

'Lori!' The name was a sound of shock. 'Are you crying—really crying, I mean?'

Strong fingers closed over her chin, twisting her face round to meet his searching gaze. One hand touched her cheek gently and came away wet.

'I don't believe it,' Hal said shakenly. 'I've never seen you cry before, not like this.'

Suddenly he pulled her close, his arms warm and strong around her. His action shattered the last shreds of Laurel's self-control and, abandoning the resolve she had so newly formed, she collapsed against him, her hands twisting in his shirt as she sobbed helplessly.

'For God's sake, Lori, what is it?' Hal's concern was the last straw. She had vowed to keep her distance, but instead her weak tears had drawn him to her. Mutely she shook her head, incapable of speech.

If only he knew how much this meant to her, how much she loved the feel of his arms around her, the warm strength of his shoulder under her cheek, the scent of his body in her nostrils. She didn't know which was worse, the searing desire that made her whole body ache or the raw, agonising pain where her heart should be.

When Hal led her into the living-room and sat her down on the settee Laurel followed him automatically like a mindless robot, incapable of thought. He knelt in front of her, cupping her face in both his hands, his eyes fixed on her face.

'Was it what I said? If it was, I'm sorry.' He laid his forehead against hers, closing his eyes. 'Darling, I'm sorry,' he murmured huskily.

The room seemed to spin round Laurel. *Darling,* he had said, the term of endearment somehow more shocking than any of his biting taunts had ever been. Was it possible——? The tiny, fragile hope vanished under a wave of despair. This was just the sort of thing she must not let happen. With an effort that tore at her heart she pulled herself free from Hal's arms.

'No, it wasn't what you said——'

'Then what is it? Please——' Hal's voice deepened, became husky. 'Tell me!'

It would have taken a far harder heart than Laurel possessed to resist that appeal. She intended just to say that talking about her parents had made her remember, give him just enough to let him know that he wasn't to blame for her distress, but once she started it all came flowing out—how lost she had felt, how alone. She didn't stop, couldn't stop to think about avoiding any mention of Jenny or Lorraine, but in the end it wasn't necessary. It was her own loss, her own pain and fear at the thought of the task her father had left her she was talking about as she had never spoken of it before, not even to Barbara, because Barbara had come into her life months later when she had believed she was healed. Now she found she had never fully healed, the wound had only been covered over lightly until talking to Hal had wrenched it open again.

Hal had taken her in his arms again. She heard his voice offering comfort, soothing her until the storm had passed and she was calm again. But it was the calm of desperation, and those soothing words twisted like a knife turning painfully in her already desolated heart. Because it was worse than before, because this time his sympathy was for *her*, Lorraine had nothing to do with it, and she felt she couldn't bear to have Hal so very close knowing that in reality they were still light years apart.

Hal was kissing her face, soft, brief kisses brushing away her tears; bittersweet caresses that plunged the knife in even deeper as they roused that sweet sensual longing in her once more. He moved to sit beside her and it felt so right and natural to have him there, his arms around her, that, although she knew she should move away, end this before it went any further, she didn't have the strength to move, her body had turned traitor to her and refused to obey even the weak commands she tried to force on it. And when Hal's mouth covered her own thought too vanished and she responded willingly to his kisses, unable to think of any other possible reaction.

But when Hal's hand slid inside the open neck of her shirt to stroke the soft curve of her breast an electric impulse of sheer panic registered in Laurel's bruised mind, her eyes flew open and she lifted a hand to his to still its caressing movement. There was a sour taste in her mouth, a queasy, sickening feeling in the pit of her stomach. She could not let any man make love to her when it was all a lie—and particularly not Hal, the man she loved. She was shaking with fear, but this was a new and very different fear from the one that had made her afraid of discovery. She was no longer afraid that if Hal made love to her he would find out that she was not Lorraine—on the contrary, she was terrified that he would *not* discover that she was someone very different. She couldn't bear to be made love to in her sister's place.

'Hal——' she began, but could not go on. Her mouth was dry and she knew that the lean brown fingers still resting lightly over her heart must feel its erratic, uneven pounding. 'Hal—please——' she tried again, but his lips brushed over hers, silencing her.

'I know,' Hal murmured against her mouth. 'Don't worry, my lovely, I understand.'

He lifted his head to regard her seriously, his hand moving up inside her shirt to close over her shoulder.

'It's different this time, isn't it?' he said soberly. 'I'm not sure quite how it's different, but it is. Sometimes I'm not even sure you're the woman I married. Maybe I've changed too, I don't know, but there's something that wasn't there the last time, and I know you feel it too.'

'Yes,' Laurel whispered weakly, trying to drag up the strength to think. That 'I'm not even sure you're the woman I married' had devastated her. Her heart screamed at her to tell Hal the truth, while cold, unhappy reason warned that that was something she must never do. 'But——' She didn't know how she would have gone on, but Hal laid his hand across her lips to silence her.

'Sssh! Leave it now, Lori,' he said gently. 'It's all too new; let's not rush it. God knows where this is leading, but I'm prepared to go with the tide and see what happens.'

He glanced down at Laurel's upturned face where it rested against his shoulder and his blue eyes warmed suddenly, like the sea when the sun touches it, his smile sending a searing flare of agony through her raw nerves.

'It might not last, but we'll take what there is—and I promise you one thing.' His hand left her shoulder and touched her face with breathtaking gentleness, his smile taking on a wryly regretful twist. 'I won't pressurise you this time—we got caught that way before. We'll take all the time we need to get to know each other and, who knows, there may be a future for us after all.'

Laurel had thought she was beyond feeling any more pain, but the sound of Hal's words was like an icy blast that froze her heart in a solid block of ice. It was the bitterest, the most savage irony that Hal should start to think that perhaps they had a future together just when she had admitted once and for all that such a thing could never be.

CHAPTER EIGHT

As THE TAXI pulled up outside Highcliff Laurel was stunned to see a light shining through a crack in the curtains of the living-room. Surely Hal couldn't be home already?

No—he had told her he had business to attend to in London. He had a meeting arranged with his agent, so he was staying overnight before driving back to Nunham with Adele and Simon. He was unlikely to be back before lunch time tomorrow. In the darkness Laurel recalled bitterly how she had viewed the actress's visit as something of a godsend. Hal would be forced to spend time with his guests, leaving him little opportunity to be alone with her—and that was the only way she could think of coping with the position in which she now found herself. If she was going to see this thing through—and the events of the day had driven home to her that she *had* to see it through—then the less time she spent with Hal the better.

Having paid her fare, Laurel let herself into the house and stood in the hall, listening for any sound of occupation. Nothing. Probably Jan had called round and, having seen the note she had left explaining that she would be away all day, had left a light or two on as a precaution against burglars—a wise move, considering Highcliff's isolated position. She must remember to thank the the housekeeper for her forethought; she hadn't looked forward to returning to a dark and silent house, especially when it would seem so empty without Hal.

Not that she had had much time to be aware of Hal's absence. As soon as she had heard his car drive away she had hurried downstairs to phone for a taxi to take her to the railway station.

Wearily Laurel pushed a hand through the coppery fall of her hair, her green eyes clouded with tiredness and despair. It had been a long, exhausting day, the journeys to and from Ashingby an ordeal in the almost overpowering heat, but her fatigue was more mental than physical, the result of going over and over the same ground and coming up with no answer other than the one she already knew to be her only possible choice. And things had been made worse by the fact that she had slept so little last night.

Hal had kept to his promise to put no pressure on her and had carefully opted to sleep in another room, leaving her alone in his bedroom.

'I'll be leaving at some ungodly hour in the morning anyway,' he had added with a smile that wrenched at her heart. 'I wouldn't want to disturb you when I get up.'

But as things had turned out he wouldn't have disturbed her at all. Well before he had left the house she had been up and dressed, ready for her journey to Ashingby. During the night her half-formed plan to visit Jenny while Hal was in London had come to appear as the only possible move she could make. She desperately needed to see Jenny, knowing that only by reinforcing to herself the seriousness of the little girl's plight could she find the strength to go through with what remained of the two months Hal had asked of her.

When she had believed Hal to be the uncaring monster Lorraine had described she had been able to justify her actions only by balancing Jenny's very real needs against his purely selfish desire to possess the woman he had married. Her own growing love for him had complicated matters greatly, but her commitment to her sister had outweighed any needs of her own, particularly when she had known that, even if she had declared how she felt, Hal would never love her in return.

But now, with her new understanding of Hal's character and when it seemed likely that the thing she most longed for and yet dreaded might be happening, if Hal really cared, even the slightest bit, for her as a person, then what she was doing could never be regarded in the terms of a business deal. To take Hal's money and leave at the end of the two months without a thought for his feelings was an act so callous that she shuddered to contemplate it. But what was the alternative? Despairingly, Laurel had admitted to herself that she did not think there was one.

And so she had set out for Ashingby, and from the moment she saw Jenny's face she recognised the hopelessness of even considering any course of action other than the one she had originally planned. The little girl was bubbling with excitement, having just been told that the she would be fit to travel very soon.

'Doctor Griffin says my back won't hurt any more when it's mended,' Jenny declared happily, totally unaware of the way every word she spoke aggravated Laurel's distress. 'And then my legs will work properly and if I do my exercises every day I'll be able to dance again. Doctor Griffin says that I'll be Alice in the next concert, not just the Dormouse!'

Laurel caught her breath painfully. She had almost convinced herself that the only thing she could do was to tell Hal the truth and throw herself on his mercy, but Jenny's happiness forced her to remember just how much was at stake. If Hal refused to help her, demanded his money back—and who could blame him if he did?— then Jenny's misery would be all the greater because of the hope she felt now. It was a terrible irony that, in the moment when she should be experiencing her greatest joy, with Jenny's future all but assured, all she could think of was how much she stood to lose.

'Auntie Babs says I should write a letter to Mr Rochester to thank him for helping me,' Jenny was saying. 'Do you think I should, Lauri?'

Laurel paled at the thought. Just what Hal's reaction would be if a letter from Jenny arrived she could not imagine.

'Don't you worry your head about that, love,' she said hastily. 'I'll thank him for you.' Her voice cracked on the words. She couldn't even do that! Couldn't even *thank* Hal properly. How was she ever to live with herself after this? 'All you have to do is to rest and get well and strong. Promise me you'll do everything the doctors tell you.'

'All right.' Jenny's voice was dull, her face paling as she came to the end of her small store of energy. 'But, Lauri, I don't want to rest! I'm tired of being in bed! I want to get up!'

'I know, poppet.' Laurel's heart ached at the longing in her sister's voice. 'But it won't be for long now. You'll just have to be patient.'

'I will get better, won't I?' The distinct tremor in Jenny's voice made tears burn in Laurel's eyes. Fiercely she blinked them away.

'Of course you'll get better, love,' she said, ruthlessly refusing to allow any note of doubt, any hint of her own worries to creep into her voice. 'Once you've had that operation you'll be good as new—better, even. If Doctor Griffin says you'll be dancing Alice then you will. He's the doctor, he should know.'

Her confident approach succeeded, within seconds Jenny's doubts were forgotten, her confidence in Laurel's ability to put everything right restored and, although she protested when her sister said she had to go, she was easily persuaded by the argument that Laurel had a lot to do to ensure that the operation went ahead as planned.

When Laurel turned for a last look at her small sister Jenny had already picked up her tap-dancing shoes and was stroking them lovingly. That picture stayed with Laurel throughout the long, draining journey home. Jenny's dream of being able to dance again was the one thing that had sustained her throughout her ordeal— and would sustain her during the weeks to come—she could never deprive the little girl of the future that now stretched ahead of her so brightly, full of golden promise.

But what about herself? She still had to face up to the fact that she had to choose between the two people she loved most in all the world—Jenny and Hal—and deep in her heart she knew she could not choose Hal. Even as her heart cried out against the thought of continuing to deceive him, Laurel knew that that was what she had to do. If Hal continued to believe that she was Lorraine she might still salvage something from this appalling situation. The way to hurt him the least was to make sure that he never knew the truth. Surely it was better for him to believe that the wife he had had such contempt for had behaved in the callous, mercenary way he expected of her than to let him suspect even for a moment that another woman had deceived him, deliberately taking his wife's place in order to take the money he had offered.

But if she was to ensure that Hal went on believing she was Lorraine, she was going to have to be very much more careful. Her love for Hal had made her respond to him in a way that had clearly disconcerted and troubled him; from now on she would have to keep a much tighter grip on her feelings. She would have to *be* Lorraine—and the Lorraine Hal had expected at that first meeting—and it would have to be the performance of a lifetime.

'Where the hell have you been?' A voice, harsh and rough, intruded violently into her thoughts and Laurel's eyes, wide with shock, flew to a suddenly open doorway to stare in blank amazement at the tall, dark figure who stood silhouetted against the light from the living-room.

No! It couldn't be! Her eyes were playing tricks on her because she was so tired. She blinked hard to clear her vision, but when she looked again Hal was still there, and there was no denying the reality of the savage voice when he spoke again.

'Well? Did you hear me? I want to know where the hell you've been until now.'

'I——' Shock had dried Laurel's throat, depriving her of the ability to speak, and she swallowed convulsively, still staring at this man who must be Hal and yet looked so very different.

The fawn suit which he wore with a bronze-coloured shirt looked as if it must have been tailored on to him to account for the perfection of its fit, its elegance stunning when she was used to the casual denim jeans and T-shirts he wore when at Highcliff. He must somehow have found the time to have his hair cut in London, for its dark disorder had been replaced by sleek and obviously expensive styling, and as he took a step towards her the tangy scent of aftershave reached her nostrils. He looked stylish, well-groomed, the Hal of London and his wealthy, socialite friends, obviously a man of power and money. And now she knew just why Lorraine had rushed into a marriage she was to regret later. *This* man would have swept her off her feet, she wouldn't have been able to resist the aura of wealth and authority that surrounded him. But, even as her stomach contracted on a wave of fear as she saw the hard, inimical set to his mouth, the light of cold anger in his eyes, Laurel's heart ached for the wild pirate she had first seen.

But what was Hal doing here? Why was he at Highcliff when he was supposed to be staying in London? And what had made him so terribly, savagely angry?

'Well?'

The single syllable was ominously threatening and, hearing it, Laurel couldn't help reflecting that, once again, this situation had a terrible bitter irony. She had forced herself to accept that she would have to distance herself from Hal somehow and had spent the journey home wondering just how she was going to manage to do it. Now it seemed that fate had taken a hand and, to judge by Hal's tone and expression, she need do nothing at all. The distance was already there, though she had no idea what had caused it.

'*Where have you been?*' Hal hadn't raised his voice, but the words came with the force of bullets from a gun.

'I—I've been out.' Foolish and inane as it sounded, it was all Laurel could manage.

'I can see that!' He dismissed her stumbling words with contempt. 'But it's now twelve o'clock and I've been sitting here, waiting, for hours. I think you owe me an explanation.'

'You've been——' If he'd been waiting for hours as he said then that possibly explained his anger—but Laurel had the uneasy suspicion there was more to it than that. 'When did you get back?'

'Around nine. Lorraine——'

Hal's use of her twin's name had the effect of a splash of cold water in Laurel's face, clearing her thoughts. He had to believe that she was Lorraine—for his own sake—and her sister would never have put up with this sort of questioning without fighting back. With a strength born of desperation Laurel managed to lift her head and meet those cold blue eyes defiantly.

'I don't know what all the fuss is about. You left me on my own all day, surely I'm entitled to visit my——'

Hot colour flooded her face as she caught up the betraying word 'sister' and she came perilously close to losing her precarious grip on her self-control at the thought that, in Hal's eyes, that blush would look like a sign of guilt.

'—a *friend*—in hospital,' she added hastily, the small gesture towards the truth doing nothing to appease her outraged conscience.

Hal lifted a hand and looked ostentatiously at the gold watch on his wrist.

'I never knew Marborough General had such extended visiting hours,' he drawled with a biting satire that had Laurel flinching as if each word had been a drop of acid landing on her sensitive skin.

'Oh, the hospital isn't in Marborough—it's—somewhere else.'

She nerved herself for the inevitable question, trying frantically to think of some other town she could name when Hal demanded to know exactly where the hospital was. But, surprisingly, the question never came. Instead he lapsed into a brooding silence, his eyes concealed under hooded lids so that she could read nothing of his thoughts in them. His silence stretched Laurel's nerves to breaking-point until at last she had to speak or scream.

'Why are you back so early, Hal?' It took a determined effort, but she managed to keep her voice from shaking although, tautly controlled, it sounded cold and brittle. 'And where are Adele and Simon?'

Were they in the living-room, beyond that open door? Had they heard everything Hal had said? If so, they were hardly likely to believe that Hal and his wife were reconciled, which was what he had once declared to be his aim in this unbelievable partnership.

'Adele?' The word came vaguely as if Hal had dragged his mind away from other, very different thoughts. 'She's still in London—Simon too——' His mouth twisted savagely. 'I asked them not to come this weekend.'

'You——' Laurel could scarcely believe she had heard him right. 'But why?'

The shaky question had the effect of pressing a switch on a detonator.

'*Why?*' he exploded, his face suddenly white with fury, harsh lines etched around his nose and mouth and white-hot flames of anger flaring in the darkness of his eyes. 'I'll tell you why! I promised you time—time for both of us to get to know each other——' His hard, mirthless laugh was a shocking sound in the stillness of the night. 'I thought we'd have a better chance on our own, without anyone else around, so I told Simon and Adele it wasn't convenient for them to come this weekend. Then I rushed through the things I had to do and came back.'

Once more that harsh laughter caught on Laurel's raw nerves so that she wanted to cry out, beg him to stop.

'I drove like a maniac to get here and then I find——' For the first time Hal's voice rose above a savage monotone. 'I find you're out—visiting a *friend*!'

He spat the last word in Laurel's face in a tone of such violent loathing that instinctively she flinched away.

'Well? Nothing to say, Lori?'

Nothing to say? What *could* she say? Laurel felt as if the acid had reached her heart, shrivelling it inside her. Hal had asked his guests to stay in London and had hurried back to Nunham—and the only possible explanation for his actions was that he was trying to make things work, that he had wanted to be at Highcliff, with her.

No, with *Lorraine*. The bitterness of the realisation was unbearable, and Laurel folded her arms around her body as if to keep herself from falling apart. The suit, the shirt, even that damned haircut were all deliberately planned to please her twin—— But it was with *Laurel* that Hal had achieved a sort of understanding before the trip to London.

Laurel clenched her hands into tight fists, her nails digging into her palms, trying to use the small, physical pain to distract herself from the tearing anguish inside her. Lorraine or Laurel, what did it matter? She couldn't let that fragile understanding continue; she had to destroy it, for Jenny's sake—and for Hal's.

'And what about Max?' she asked, snatching at the one thing she could think of that would turn the conversation from the dangerous path it was taking. 'Did you cancel his visit too?' The recollection of her earlier belief that the expected visitors would distract Hal, prevent him from having much time alone with her, put a new intensity into her voice. How would she cope if Max too were to stay away?

She would have thought it was impossible for Hal to lose any more colour, but his skin appeared almost transparent, it was stretched so tightly across the hard bones of his face.

'Max?' The name hissed between clenched teeth. 'Oh no, *he* will turn up when it suits him—you know Max.'

There was an emphasis on the final comment that reminded Laurel of the telephone conversation she had overheard, and Hal's reaction when he discovered that Max was on the other end of the line. But Max's relationship with the other man wasn't her primary concern. Right now, all she could think of was getting away, going upstairs to her bedroom before she broke down completely.

'So we still have one visitor coming.' Why had Hal not cancelled Max's visit as well if he wanted to be alone with her? Perhaps he hadn't been able to get in touch with him. One man, particularly one he appeared to dislike, might not distract Hal as much as she had hoped his other friends would, but he would at least provide some sort of a buffer between them, and for that she had to be grateful. 'In that case, I hope you don't mind if I go to bed. It's very late and I—— Oh!'

She had moved towards the stairs as she spoke but broke off in alarm as Hal's hand flashed out and fastened around her arm, jerking her to a halt with a violence that brought a gasping cry to her lips.

'Oh, no, you don't!' he snarled. 'You don't just walk out on me like that!'

Suddenly, shockingly, his face changed, a touch of colour coming back into his cheeks, the narrow slash of his mouth softening, his eyes darkening swiftly as, in a gesture so slow, so mechanical it was almost as if he didn't know what he was doing, as if his hand had moved of its own volition, he reached out and touched the red-gold strands of her hair with a dreamlike softness.

'You little witch,' he murmured, his voice thick and blurred. 'From the moment I saw those enticing green eyes and that glorious body of yours I've been under your spell, and I can't get free. I wish to God I could, but you're in my blood; when you're around I can't see anyone else. You're in my mind every second of the day. I can't think straight, can't keep from wanting you, so I have to work like a lunatic to keep from going completely insane.'

His eyes swept down over her body, lingering on the soft curves under the thin white cotton of her dress, and he gave a deep, ragged sigh.

'Now I'm not even sure I want to be free,' he went on unevenly, his breathing quickening noticeably, his grip on her arm loosening, changing subtly from a restraint to a caress.

'Hal——' Laurel tried shakily, but her voice died in her throat and she could only stand silently, mesmerised by the dark intensity of his gaze.

Another of those terrible laughs, a dreadful sound of disgust and self-derision, splintered the silence, and the next moment she was pulled hard against the wall of Hal's chest, held by a furious, hurtful strength so that she had no chance of escape as his lips came down hard on hers.

There was nothing sensual or arousing about the way he kissed her, it was a kiss of cold passion, meant to punish, to degrade, but in spite of that she still felt the sudden upsurge of yearning need that drove all resistance from her, left her weak and pliant against him, prepared to take anything—even this travesty of a kiss.

She felt Hal's sudden shock as he sensed the softening of her mouth, heard his deep groan, and hardly recognised his voice, husky with need and something close to despair as he muttered against her lips, 'God, Lori, what is it you do to me?'

And you to me, Laurel answered him in the privacy of her thoughts, knowing that, with that one touch of his lips, even with a kiss used as a weapon, he had driven all her careful resolutions from her mind, leaving her functioning only on pure instinct, an instinct that drove her to link her arms around his neck, curve her body against his, and open her lips to his exploring tongue when his kiss changed to one of warm sensuality as his hands slid down her back to hold her at the base of her spine so that every part of her, breast, hips, thighs, was aware of the heat of his skin even through the material of his clothes.

'Dear God, but I want you!' Hal's breath shivered across her skin as his mouth slid down the column of her throat and down towards the curves of her breasts above the low-cut, lace-edged neckline of her dress. Her blood felt white-hot in her veins, even her bones seeming to melt in the heat of her need, her flesh ached to be caressed and she could not hold back a cry of delight when his hands moved to cover her breasts, the arousing movements of his thumbs making her shudder convulsively.

The need to feel more of him was overwhelming and, her fingers clumsy in their haste, she tugged at the buttons of his shirt, his hoarse cry of pleasure echoing in her head as she slid her hands across his chest, glorying in the tremor of response that shook him.

'Oh, my God—Lorraine!' he groaned, and the sound of the name that wasn't her own penetrated the haze of desire that filled Laurel's mind, jarring her back to reality with a sickening jolt.

This was what she could not let happen, what she had vowed must *never* happen. There could be no closeness between Hal and herself—*ever*. With a wrench that tore at her heart she twisted her head, pulling her mouth away from his.

'*No!* Hal, no! You promised you wouldn't pressurise me——'

For a second, seeing the black, murderous rage in his eyes, she thought he was going to ignore her plea, and as his fingers tightened on her arms she knew with bitter despair that if he so much as kissed her again she would be lost, unable, in spite of the consequences, to refuse him what she too wanted so much.

'Hal, please——' she tried again, and at last the bruising grip on her arms loosened fractionally.

'Yes, of course—I promised. And an honourable man always keeps his promises.'

The dark cynicism was like a stunning blow to the head and his hands were snatched away so swiftly that for a moment Laurel didn't realise she was free.

'No pressure, Lori,' he said, and the blank flatness of his tone tore at her heart. 'I'll keep my word, but I'm only human, so don't push me or I won't be answerable for the consequences.' He rubbed the back of his hand across his eyes in a tired, angry, and unconsciously vulnerable gesture that had Laurel fighting back tears she didn't dare let him see. 'If you're wise you'll go to bed now, while you still can.'

It was the greatest foolishness, she knew, but she couldn't leave him—not like this.

'Hal——' she began tremulously, then stopped in shock as he flung up his hands defensively.

'Don't you know when to stop?' he snarled at her. 'Don't you know how close I am to flinging you on the floor and taking you right here and now, promise or no promise? For God's sake, Lori, leave me alone!'

Heedless of her white, unhappy face and tear-filled eyes, he caught hold of her again and turned her roughly, pushing her towards the stairs.

'I can't take any more of you tonight. If you've any sense you'll go now before I do something I really regret. But there's one thing I pray, Lori, and that's that one day you'll know what it feels like to be rejected as you've constantly rejected me—though I doubt if that cold little heart of yours has enough feeling in it to care!'

He flung the last words over his shoulder as he headed towards the living-room and a moment later the door slammed to behind him.

As the tension which was all that had been keeping her on her feet drained from Laurel's body she found she had barely enough strength to drag herself upstairs and into her room. There, she sank down on to the bed and abandoned herself to her tears, weeping with harsh, racking sobs that shook her whole body. She had done it. She had driven Hal so far away from her that he would never want to come back to her even if she went down on her knees and begged him.

She had *had* to do it; it was the only way, but it was the hardest thing she had ever done in her life, and her heart felt as if it would burst under the pressure of all the pain that was in it. With a choking cry of despair she lay back on the bed, hugging a pillow tightly up against her, holding it close as if it were Hal himself.

CHAPTER NINE

THE BEACH was very beautiful in the stillness of the afternoon, its sand smooth and golden with the soft blue-green of the sea breaking into white, foaming waves as it washed against the shore. But Laurel was blind to the attractions of her surroundings as she stood with her shoulders hunched despondently, staring sightlessly at the distant horizon.

At the far end of the small bay a young couple had set up deckchairs and a windbreak, and a few yards away from Laurel their young daughter paddled happily in the sea with much splashing and cries of delighted laughter, but Laurel couldn't bear to look at her. The small, sturdy frame, bright eyes and wide smile reminded her unbearably of Jenny in the days before her accident, though the blonde curls were so very different from her little sister's mop of bright red hair, and each shriek of laughter stabbed like a white-hot knife straight into her heart. So she kept her eyes carefully averted, fixed on the sea in spite of the way its colour reminded her of Hal's eyes, tormenting her with the memory of the way those eyes had hardened last night, filling with a mixture of cold anger, rejection and bitter disgust.

Laurel rubbed the back of her hand across her forehead, wishing she could erase those painful memories, though she knew that nothing would ever remove the scene of the previous night from her mind. It would always be there, haunting her, and she could only pray that time would at least dull the pain, for she would never be completely free of it. There was a bruised ache deep inside her where her heart should be. It was true, then, she thought miserably, your heart could feel a real, physical pain, nothing sharp or acute but a continual, nagging discomfort, unless she probed too deeply and roused the bitter, searing anguish that was always just below the surface.

'Even on the darkest night of your life you can always chase the dawn.' The phrase from Hal's novel, his grandmother's saying, echoed over and over in her head. Last night had certainly seemed like the darkest night of her life, but when all this was over, when the two months were up, would she ever be able to find the hope of a new dawn, ever manage to be happy without Hal? She felt a great empathy with Maria, understanding as she never would have done before just how she had felt when she fell in love with a man she had only known for a few days, and, like Maria, she too would have to face a future without the man to whom she had given her heart.

Laurel started as a cold wet nose was pushed into the palm of her hand.

'Oh, Jet!' With a cry that was a mixture of delight and a choking sob, she turned to the dog who, with his cut paw now well healed, had come up behind her, his tail wagging furiously as she patted his sleek black head. 'I'm going to miss you so much when I've gone!'

'Only Jet?'

The sardonic voice behind her had her swinging round violently and her heart began to race at the sight of Hal's tall, dark figure only a few feet away from her. With an effort she caught back a cry of shock that almost escaped her as she saw how drawn and tense he looked, his blue eyes shadowed and lines of fatigue and strain etched around his nose and mouth. But, dressed in jeans and a faded denim shirt, his hair windblown and tousled, he was once more the wild pirate she had first met, no longer the sleekly alien city man, and her heart twisted with longing at the sight of him.

She could find no words to answer his question, her tongue seemed to have stuck to the roof of her mouth, but Hal appeared to need no response as he went on, with an inclination of his head towards Jet who was now rolling on his back, his paws in the air, in the hope Laurel would rub his stomach in the way he loved, 'Look at that dog—he has no doubts, he trusts you completely—but then you've never deceived him, have you, Lori?'

The stark, unemotional words seemed to hang in the air between them as Laurel's nerves clenched in panic as for one terrifying moment she thought that he had somehow found out or guessed at the truth. But a swift glance into those clouded eyes revealed none of the savage anger she might have expected if he had, only a complete blanking off of all emotion that was infinitely more disturbing than any dark fury.

So was he simply referring to the previous night, or to something else, something Lorraine had done? Laurel flinched away from thoughts of her twin, unable in her present intensely vulnerable state of mind to cope with them, particularly with Hal so very close, the taut, antagonistic set of his head and shoulders indicating his mood only too clearly.

'You'll drive me mad yet,' he muttered bitterly. 'You're so beautiful—you look so innocent, so honest on the outside, but inside——'

Even as his lips twisted in disgust his hand was reaching out as if it had a mind of its own to stroke her hair, his fingers tangling in the rich copper mane.

'Hal——'

Laurel's lips felt frozen, too stiff to speak properly, and the word came out on a hoarse croak, but whether in rejection of his caress or encouragement even Laurel herself couldn't tell, and she had no idea how she would have continued if at that moment the calm of the afternoon hadn't been shattered by a high, piercing scream of panic.

Whirling round, Laurel saw that the little girl she had seen paddling earlier on had wandered rather too far into the sea and had slipped and fallen. Even though she was still in fairly shallow water the weight of her sodden dress made it impossible for her to get to her feet and the pull of the undercurrent was dragging her further out from the shore. At the far end of the beach her father was already on his feet, but he was much further away from the terrified child than either Hal or Laurel.

It took just a split second for Laurel to take in the situation, then she pulled away from Hal in the same moment that he released her and began to run, splashing through the waves with total disregard for any damage she might do the brand-new cream cotton trousers and matching silky top she wore, even though they had cost a small fortune when Hal had insisted she bought them during that hateful shopping expedition. Her heart racing, she reached the little girl in minutes, grabbing her just as she let out another panic-stricken scream. But in spite of her size the child was no lightweight and the pull of the current threatened to tug her out of Laurel's grasp. She knew a second of despair, then strong brown hands closed around the little girl's waist, she saw the muscles in Hal's tanned arms tighten and a minute later the child was safe, held well above the water, close against Hal's chest.

'Oh, thank God!'

Unthinkingly Laurel turned to smile her relief straight at Hal's face, and the ground seemed to tilt under her feet as she saw her own feelings mirrored in his eyes in a moment of sharing so intense that it made her breath catch in her throat. Then he turned his attention to the child, soothing her with quiet comforting words, and from being so totally one they were once again two separate people, leaving Laurel feeling terribly alone and bereft at the thought of everything that kept them so far apart.

The little girl's screams had faded to hiccuping sobs as her father reached their side, his face pale with shock, words of gratitude pouring from his lips as he took his daughter into his arms.

'I don't know how to thank you. I only took my eyes off her for a moment——'

'She's fine,' Hal reassured him. 'I don't think her head went under the water at all. She's had a nasty fright, nothing more. She'll be OK in a minute.'

As if to prove his point, the little girl's sobs ceased and she managed a wavering smile for her rescuers.

'All the same, I just can't thank you enough. Annie's been told not to go into the sea, to stay right on the edge, but of course you know what five-year-olds are like.'

Laurel almost nodded automatic agreement, but realised what she had been about to do and caught herself up just in time, pushing a hand through her hair to cover her unease so that the sunlight glinted on the thick gold band around her finger, drawing the man's eyes to it.

'Do you have any children of your own?'

'No.' It was Hal who spoke; Laurel, her mind full of the thoughts of Jenny that had almost led her to give too much away, was incapable of speech. 'We don't—but I have to admit that I'd dearly love a daughter, especially if she was anything like this little charmer.'

Laurel's gaze flew to his face as he reached out and ruffled Annie's golden curls, her thoughts reeling as she saw in his eyes a depth of feeling that told her without any shadow of doubt that his words were not just casual conversation but strongly and sincerely meant.

Would he have looked like that if he'd seen Jenny? If she had shown him a photograph of her little sister, would his face have softened in this way? Surely *this* Hal would have done anything in his power to save any child from pain and unhappiness, just as he had dashed to Annie's rescue, his reaction as instinctive as her own. Bitter anguish seared through Laurel at the thought that if only she had had the courage to tell Hal the whole truth at the beginning, using the picture of Jenny she always carried with her to reinforce her story, then he might have been only too willing to help, probably without any conditions at all. But, misled by Lorraine's story, she had convinced herself he would never listen.

Through a fog of misery Laurel vaguely heard Annie's father's parting words and saw him carry his daughter away, but all the time, superimposed on the scene before her, she saw an image of Hal's face and the open emotion on it as he looked at the little girl.

'You're soaked.' Hal's voice broke into her thoughts, his matter-of-fact comment strangely shocking to Laurel in her hypersensitive frame of mind. 'In fact we both are. We'd better go inside and get changed.'

Laurel turned towards the path that led up to Highcliff in the automatic response of a robot programmed to do as Hal said, her mind too full of private thoughts to allow her to make any decisions of her own. On her previous visit to the beach she had managed the steep climb to the house without any great effort, but this time the shock of Annie's accident and Hal's reaction to it seemed to have drained all her energy and she found it a struggle, slipping frequently in the fine sand until Hal, just ahead of her, noticed her difficulties and silently reached out a hand to help her. After a second's hesitation she grasped his fingers with her own, tiny flames of reaction flickering in her veins at the feel of his hand on hers, the small contact giving her the courage to try and speak what was on her mind.

'Did you mean what you said about wanting a daughter of your own?'

Hal's steady stride didn't alter, but she felt the swift tightening of the muscles in his hand before he spoke.

'You know I did.' He didn't look at her and his tone was tight and rough-edged. 'You know how much I've always envied Teresa those nephews of mine.'

Something about the way he spoke the name left Laurel with the impression that he expected that Lorraine would have recognised it, but other thoughts crowded in on her mind so fast that she had no time to pause to consider the implications of that fact. Was this what had caused the break-up? She could well imagine that Lorraine, who had adamantly refused to have anything to do with Jenny, her face a picture of disgust at the thought of changing a single nappy, would have been unlikely to want a baby of her own, and if Hal—who had already demonstrated how much his family meant to him by the way he had talked of his grandmother— had longed for children of his own then she could see how that would have driven her sister and her husband apart.

But if Hal had always wanted a child then perhaps there was a fragile chance that she could extricate herself from this web of deceit after all. He might hate her for what she had done, but surely he would want to help *Jenny*. Laurel prayed that he would because, after that moment of intense sharing, of total empathy, she knew she couldn't carry her burden of lies and deception any longer. Drawing a deep breath, she had opened her mouth to speak, to tell Hal everything, when above them, at the top of the cliff, a man's voice spoke casually.

'So this is where you've got to! You surprise me, Hal— I expected to find a workaholic like you at your desk, not wasting time on the beach.' The drawling tones were laced with a mockery that set Laurel's teeth on edge at once.

As she trudged up the last few feet of the path the sun was shining straight into her eyes so that the man before her was simply a dark blur and she was unable to make out any of his features, but she felt the tightening of Hal's grip on her hand, could sense the tension in every inch of his body, and her own nerves prickled in response.

'Max,' said Hal curtly, nodding a distant greeting. 'I wasn't expecting you so early.'

So *this* was Max, the man Lorraine was supposed to know, a man whom, it was obvious from his tone during the telephone call she had overheard and his reaction now, Hal did not like at all. Then, as the man moved a step or two backwards out of the line of the sun, Laurel saw him clearly for the first time and with a strong sense of foreboding recognised him at once.

The man Hal had called Max looked very much as he had done in the photograph Laurel had found in Lorraine's suitcase. The thick fair hair had been bleached by some time in the sun, as his tanned skin testified, his clothes were more casual now, a short-sleeved shirt and jeans, but still with a style that spoke of money, and the signs of self-indulgence which the photograph had mercifully blurred were rather more pronounced, but Laurel could be in no doubt that this was the same man. But why had Lorraine had his photograph with her? What was this man to her twin?

Her breath came quickly and unevenly, her palms damp with perspiration. Would Max too believe she was Lorraine, or had the moment she had been dreading finally arrived? One word from Max and her position would be exposed for the lie it was without any chance to explain to Hal about Jenny.

Until that moment she had been hidden behind Hal, but now as he took a step forward Max noticed her and she saw his start of surprise.

'Lorraine!'

The single word calmed Laurel's racing pulse. Max's tone had revealed nothing beyond evident surprise at her presence. But then she looked like Lorraine, she was here with Hal, who clearly considered her to be his wife, so there was no reason at all for Max to suspect she was anyone else, particularly not if Lorraine had told him that she had no family as she had told Hal.

'You're the last person I would have expected to see here,' Max went on in a stunned voice, his gaze going to Laurel's hand, still linked with Hal's, as if he couldn't believe the evidence of his own eyes. 'Why——?' He seemed at a loss for words.

'Lori's staying for a while until we—sort things out,' Hal said quietly, but there was a strange note in his voice and his grip tightened on her hand. It seemed almost as if he wanted to claim her as his in front of Max, as if he was warning off anyone who might try to invade his territory, and only now, as her fears of being exposed as a fake subsided, did Laurel realise how intently he was watching her and Max, his sea-coloured eyes noting every flicker of reaction. Dear God, had Lorraine and Max been more than friends? Was that why Hal disliked the other man so much? But in that case why had he invited Max to Highcliff?

Max seemed to have recovered some of his composure. 'It's good to see you,' he said to Laurel. 'You're looking—well.'

His momentary hesitation made Laurel painfully aware of her own appearance. With her hair in wild disarray after her dash to Annie's rescue and her sea-splashed clothes, she knew she must look very different from the well-groomed Lorraine Rochester Max had known. Automatically she put up a hand to smooth some order into her tangled locks, and found the effect of her actions on Max strongly disturbing. A sudden, smugly satisfied look came into his eyes as if he had taken her concern for her appearance to be meant for him alone. Acutely aware of Hal's watchful eyes, Laurel frowned slightly and, she hoped, discouragingly. She had more than enough on her plate already, the last thing she needed was the added complication of whatever had been between her twin and this man.

Back at the house, she took only minutes to change out of her wet clothes, then hurriedly made her way to the kitchen where she found Jan busy with preparations for dinner that evening. She needed time away from the undercurrents of tension she sensed between Hal and Max, time to draw breath and rethink her position with regard to these new and unexpected developments and the decision she had come to on the beach, and she hoped that the housekeeper could offer her some practical work to do until she was calm enough to cope. But Jan refused her offer of help, assuring her that she had everything under control.

'But you can stay and chat if you like. Why don't you put the kettle on? I'm dying for a cuppa.'

'How are you getting on with lover boy, then?' Jan asked a while later, sipping contentedly at her tea. 'Has he told you you're the most beautiful woman in the world yet?'

'Not yet.' Laurel's laugh was touched with nervousness as she recalled the look in Max's eyes when she had smoothed her hair.

'Then he's slipping.' The housekeeper's voice was tart. 'He's been here an hour already, and that's usually quite long enough for our Mr Kennington to go into his act.'

Kennington! Laurel's cup hit the saucer with a distinct crash. Her mind seemed to be spinning out of control. Max was Max *Kennington*, and the letter she had found in Lorraine's case had concerned a hotel reservation for a Mr and Mrs Kennington. Was she jumping to conclusions, or did those two facts add up to something she didn't want to believe?

That reservation had been from the weekend just before Lorraine had appeared in Ashingby. So if her twin had planned to meet Max what had gone wrong?—because something had gone wrong. Lorraine hadn't stayed

the full week at that hotel, she had been on her way to
Ashingby well before the reservation had expired. Miserably Laurel remembered how she had cursed Hal for
upsetting her twin so much that she had driven with the
total disregard for her and Jenny's safety that had caused
the fateful crash which had been the reason for Laurel's
coming to Nunham in the first place. But what if it had
been *Max* who was responsible for her sister's disturbed
state of mind?

'Hal and he don't appear to get on too well,' she
managed dully.

'They're not exactly the best of friends,' Jan agreed,
clearly choosing her words with care. 'The last time Max
was here there was a blazing row. You could hear them
shouting at each other in here—and they were in the
study.'

'What was it about?' Laurel forced herself to ask. If
Hal had known about her twin's relationship with the
other man then it explained every bit of his callous behaviour, his scathing contempt for his wife.

'I've no idea. I suspect there was some woman involved—it's what you'd expect with Maxy-boy—but it
was none of my business, so I just shut myself in here
and turned up the radio so I couldn't hear them. All I
know is that eventually Max stormed out threatening
vengeance—though things seem rather more peaceful
now.'

'I wonder,' Laurel murmured thoughtfully, recalling
Hal's tension, that coldly warning note in his voice.

'Well, as far as they will ever be,' Jan agreed wryly.
'It's just an uneasy truce. There's no love lost between
those two, they're not at all the same type. Max is a
great one for the high life—fast money, fast cars——'

And fast women? Laurel added unhappily in the
privacy of her own thoughts. What had happened to
Lorraine in the five years she had been away? Her twin
had always been selfish, greedy for the good things of

life—but had she really had an affair with another man so soon after her marriage to Hal? It was true that Lorraine had complained of Hal's neglect, but did that justify her own unfaithfulness? Laurel shook her head despairingly. She no longer knew what she believed in her sister's account of her marriage.

There was no one in the living-room when Laurel passed through it on her way upstairs to change for dinner, so she assumed that Hal and Max had already gone to their rooms. Did she dare snatch the opportunity to ring Jenny? Her small sister's existence now seemed the only thing she could cling on to while the rest of her world crumbled about her.

And if Hal heard her, well, it would be the perfect opportunity to tell him of Jenny's existence. She had had no chance to speak to him during the afternoon and, with Max around, it would be impossible to tell him anything over dinner. Her resolve to tell Hal the whole truth had hardened as a result of the things Jan had told her. If Lorraine had behaved as she suspected, she could no longer go through with playing a role that was growing more hateful to her with every second that passed.,

But the call was achieved without any interruption, and when Laurel went up to her bedroom some time later she realised why. Steam still clouded the bathroom mirror, there were two damp towels hung on the towel rail and the scent of some tangy aftershave permeated the air. Clearly Hal had already showered and changed. Her heart skipped a beat as she realised the full implications behind his use of the en-suite bathroom in this particular bedroom. He had slept in another room since his promise to put no pressure on her, but clearly he now intended that Max should believe that they were truly man and wife. The thought of the coming night sent a shiver of apprehension running down her spine, but then, reconsidering, she came to the conclusion that the change might work to her advantage. With Max a disturbing influence at the dinner-table she would have no opportunity to talk to Hal, but perhaps later, in the privacy of this room, she would have a chance to explain.

Laurel had thought long and hard about what to wear this evening. She knew that Hal had chosen the green dress with this particular dinner in mind—but that had been when he expected the Lorrimers to have been present. But with the thought of the explanation she would have to make at the end of the evening uppermost in her mind, Laurel knew she would need every ounce of confidence she possessed to see her through the evening—and the dress would be a vital boost to a morale that was rapidly becoming non-existent. So she showered and washed her hair, taking meticulous care over her make-up, all the time refusing to let herself think that her careful preparations might have another motivation, that underneath all the carefully rationalised reasoning was the tiny, fragile hope that just once more Hal would see her as the beautiful woman he had been attracted to—for the last time, probably, if his reaction when he learned how she had deceived him was as she expected.

A small spark of confidence lit up inside her as she considered her reflection in the mirror. The green dress was every bit as beautiful as she remembered and the loose coil into which she had gathered her hair, leaving just a few shining red-gold tendrils free around her face to soften the effect, gave her an added sophistication, drawing attention to her high cheekbones and the long line of her throat. It was the sort of hairstyle Lorraine, who favoured far more elaborate ways of wearing her hair, would never have chosen, she knew, admitting to herself that tonight she wanted to look as little like her twin as was possible when their two faces were almost identical.

As for her own face, she was more than satisfied with the effect achieved by a softly shimmering eyeshadow that emphasised the green of her eyes and a delicate touch of blusher high on her cheekbones. If there was a suggestion of tension in the way she held herself, an uneasy tightness around her usually soft, gentle mouth—well, she could do little about that. Perhaps a little wine would help relax her, though she doubted she would ever really relax until the truth was out in the open—which it would be in just a few hours' time. She was as ready as she would ever be, she decided, drawing a deep breath to calm the apprehensive fluttering in her stomach before heading for the door.

CHAPTER TEN

DINNER was an uncomfortable and difficult meal, with neither Hal nor Max contributing much to the conversation Laurel tried valiantly to maintain. Max in particular confined himself largely to drinking steadily, and when they finally moved into the living-room for coffee he helped himself liberally to brandy which he downed with as little concern as if it was water, his sullen, brooding expression deepening as the alcohol took effect. When Hal was called away to answer an important telephone call an awkward, uneasy silence descended, and Laurel, absorbed in private thoughts of the end of the evening and what would happen then, was only vaguely aware of Max moving to refill his glass yet again. She did not realise he had come up behind her until she was startled to feel his arm come round her shoulders, his brandy-scented breath warming her cheeks as he put his face very close to hers.

'God, but you're beautiful,' he muttered thickly, caressing the bare skin of her shoulders with clumsy fingers, his eyes half-closed. 'I've missed you, Lorraine, you can't imagine how much!'

'Max, don't!' Shocked and a little afraid, Laurel twisted away from him. What if Hal were to come in? Max's intoxicated state had dulled his reactions so that she was able to free herself quite easily, scrambling to her feet and moving away hastily. Max regarded her sulkily, his fair fringe falling forward into his eyes, making him look very much like some small child deprived of a toy he wanted.

'I know you're angry with me,' he said mournfully. 'You must hate me—but I can explain——'

'I don't hate you, Max,' Laurel said carefully. She had no idea how far this man's relationship with her twin had gone, but she didn't want to be involved in it one little bit—but Max was very drunk indeed, she would have to watch how she handled him. 'Why should I hate you?'

'You *know*.' Max sighed heavily. 'But I can put everything right—if you'll just let me kiss you!'

He lurched unsteadily towards her and Laurel backed away in alarm.

'Max, stop it! Don't be silly.'

That stopped him. He stood in the middle of the room, swaying slightly, a foolish, stunned expression on his face. Then, abruptly, he scowled darkly.

'I'm *not* silly!' he declared indignantly, his pronunciation overly precise. 'I've been waitin' for a chance to talk to you all evening.'

Laurel sighed despondently. If only Hal would come back! She was working completely in the dark with Max and had no idea what to say to him.

'Can't it wait until tomorrow?' she asked, hoping to put him off at least until he was rather more sober. She had more than enough on her mind already, and a confrontation with a totally inebriated Max was positively the last straw.

'*No!*' He was clearly in no mood to listen to reason. 'It can't wait a—'nother minute!' His eyes glittered unnaturally brightly beneath the heavy fringe.

Laurel eyed him warily, wondering if she could possibly escape out of the room. But Max was between her and the door and, drunk as he was, he was still a big man. She couldn't risk rousing his anger by making any rash moves.

'All right,' she forced herself to speak calmly, though her heart was beating high up in her throat, her pulse racing with the tension that stretched her nerves. 'What do you want to talk about?'

'Stop pretending you don't bloody well know what I'm talking about!' Max's voice rose to a shout. 'You *know* what I mean!' He pushed angrily and ineffectually at the hair that was falling into his eyes. 'I know you're mad at me because I didn't turn up for that week in London, but I couldn't get away. Damn it, Lorraine,' a note of maudlin self-pity slid into his voice, 'you don't know what it's like being tied to a wife like mine!'

'I didn't turn up for that week in London'—Max could only mean the week Lorraine had had a hotel booking for. So *that* was why she had been so distraught—it had nothing to do with Hal at all, and—— But then Max's last words hit her with an impact that made her head reel. 'You don't know what it's like being tied to *a wife like mine*.' Max Kennington was *married*! Laurel felt as if she was sinking into some dark, foul-smelling swamp. No wonder Lorraine had not told her the full truth; she hadn't wanted to admit that she was having an affair with a married man. Oh, Lorraine, what a mess you made of things—and now her twin had inherited the whole sorry situation.

'Can't we just forget that?' she ventured desperately.

'Oh, yes!' A slow, beatific smile spread over Max's face as he clearly misunderstood her question. 'Yes, darling, let's forget it ever happened.'

The smile deceived Laurel completely. Foolishly she relaxed, thinking that the crisis had passed, even managing to smile back at him. That momentary softening was all Max needed and, moving with a swiftness and sureness for which, believing him incapable of any definite action, she was totally unprepared, he grabbed her, pulling her up against him. The reek of brandy on his breath was sickening, and Laurel recoiled in disgust as he pressed his mouth greedily on hers.

'Max!' she protested angrily, trying to twist her face away from his.

'You're so beautiful!' Max moaned thickly. 'You drive me wild!'

His hands fumbled at the front of her dress, clumsily dragging at the delicate material as he pawed her breasts.

'Max, let me go!' Laurel struggled frantically in his arms. 'Take your hands off me!'

'Don't be a tease!' She quailed at the violence in Max's voice. 'You're mine—I want you so much, and you want me too. God, when I saw you here—with Hal of all people! Why the hell did you ever come back to him?'

'Because she does happen to be my wife,' a steely voice answered from behind them. 'And if you don't take your hands off her I'm liable to break your bloody neck!'

Max released Laurel and turned so swiftly that he knocked her off balance and she clung to a chair for support, her eyes going to the doorway where Hal stood, big and dark and menacing, the white silk of his shirt etched sharply against the blackness of the unlit hall behind him. How long had he been there? Had he seen her trying to fight Max off, or had he been only just in time to hear Max's last, damning words?

Seeing the scene through Hal's eyes, Laurel shivered in fear as his gaze flicked over her, his blue eyes darkening terrifyingly as they took in her dishevelled appearance with her hair tumbling in wild disarray about her shoulders, dragged out of its coil by Max's rough hands, and the front of her dress hanging crookedly, one strap completely torn away.

'Get out!' he ordered brutally.

'But Hal—— Please! It isn't what you think!'

'Out!' Hal repeated implacably, moving into the room to let her pass. 'This is between Max and myself. I'll deal with you later. If you aren't out of this room in five seconds,' he added as Laurel still hesitated, 'I swear

I'll put you over my shoulder and carry you upstairs myself.'

The look in his eyes left her in no doubt that he meant exactly what he had said, and as Max, who had slumped down into a chair and was carefully avoiding looking at her, clearly had no intention of coming to her aid she had no alternative but to obey. Hal silently watched her mount the stairs before he turned on his heel and strode back into the living-room, closing the door firmly behind him.

In the bedroom Laurel sat tensely on the bed, listening hard, but could hear no sound from the room below. She had expected raised voices, shouts, but instead there was just an ominous silence that she found far more unnerving than if she had actually heard a fight break out. She considered getting into bed, thinking longingly of the oblivion of sleep, but even though her mind and body were totally exhausted she rejected the idea. There was no chance of her actually sleeping, knowing that at some point she would have to face Hal, and, with that confrontation looming darkly ahead of her, it was probably wiser to remain fully dressed. She would be much too vulnerable with only a flimsy nightdress to cover her.

Miserably she thought back over her hopes for the evening, her foolish dreams of a quiet, peaceful time alone with Hal when she could explain everything to him and ask for his help for Jenny. Max's behaviour had destroyed her hopes; even the caring, sympathetic man she now knew Hal to be would be savagely angry after discovering the woman he believed to be his wife in another man's arms. And even if she convinced him that she wasn't Lorraine—— Laurel sighed despondently. She couldn't delude herself that Hal would even listen if she tried to explain. Her life lay in shattered ruins at her feet, her hopes, her dreams, even her memories of her twin, devastated by the discoveries she had made. The only thing she had left to hold on to was the thought that one day Jenny would be well again—though she was forced to doubt even that because she knew she could never endure what remained of the two months Hal had asked for. She couldn't live out this lie any longer.

At long last she heard heavy footsteps on the stairs and forced herself on to her feet, nerving herself for the moment when the door would open. She was trembling from head to foot when Hal finally came into the room, pausing just inside the doorway, his eyes going straight to her white, strained face.

Laurel couldn't even begin to guess at what had passed between him and Max. Hal's face was closed to her, his blue eyes hooded. The harsh lines might have been carved from stone for all the emotion they showed.

'I thought you'd be in bed,' he said at last, his casual, almost conversational tone throwing Laurel completely off balance. He didn't even appear to be angry any more.

'I—I waited in case you wanted to talk to me.'

'Talk!' The harsh laugh she had come to hate lashed her like a whip. 'And what did you want to talk about, lady? How about the weather? There's a nice safe topic if you like.'

Laurel's eyes were just wide green pools of shock and bewilderment in her ashen face. She had expected anger, the fierce, raging fury she had seen held ruthlessly in control when he had confronted Max, but this coldly flippant mood was something new, something she didn't understand and had no idea how to handle.

'Or is there something else you'd like to discuss?' Hal taunted sardonically. 'The problems involved in having affairs with two men under the same roof, perhaps?'

Numbly Laurel shook her head. 'Where's Max?' she asked dully, unable to find an answer to Hal's jibes.

'Gone,' he told her succinctly. 'I threw him out. If he's got any sense—which I doubt—he'll sleep off what he's drunk in his car and be on his way as soon as he's fit to drive. What's the matter, my lovely?' he demanded savagely, misinterpreting her unhappy expression. 'Did you want to go with him? It can easily be arranged.'

To Laurel's horror he wrenched open the wardrobe violently and began to pull her clothes out, flinging them towards her, heedless of the way they fell in a tangled heap on the floor.

'Hal, stop it!' she begged. 'Don't do this!'

'All you have to do is pack them,' the cruel voice went on. 'Come on, Lori, you know what to do, you've done it before, remember! You didn't hesitate then—just packed and went off to Max.'

'No!' There was no point in trying to explain that it had been Lorraine who had walked out; Hal was in no mood to listen. But she had to stop this terrible tirade somehow. 'Hal, please—I don't want to go with Max. He's married!'

'Of course he's bloody well married!' snarled Hal. 'You may have the convenient sort of memory that enables you to forget Teresa's existence, but I certainly don't!'

Teresa. Where had she heard that name before? Catching Laurel's worried frown, Hal clearly misinterpreted the reason for it.

'What's this? An attack of conscience? Why should you care, Lori?' His voice was suddenly soft, infinitely menacing. 'Why should you care *now*? Did it worry you before—when you walked out on me to set yourself up in your little love nest with Max? Did you spare a thought for Teresa then? Not you!' He shot Laurel a look of loathing so violent that she took a step backwards as if he had struck her. 'As always you thought only of yourself, what you wanted, and to hell with anyone else!'

And now, when she was least able to handle it, the full impact of what Hal had said earlier broke over

Laurel like a tidal wave, sweeping away the last, shattered shreds of her self-control.

Teresa. 'You know how much I've always envied Teresa those nephews of mine.' Teresa was Hal's *sister* and Max was her husband. Pieces of the jigsaw fell into place with a rapidity that made her head reel, and they built up to form an appalling picture. She had suspected that Lorraine had had an affair with Max—but not like this! Now she knew that her twin had walked out on Hal in order to be with his sister's husband!

'Oh no! *No!*'

'Oh *yes*, my lovely,' goaded Hal. 'Can't you take the truth?'

Laurel's control snapped completely. Without realising what she was doing, she lashed out at Hal, pounding with her fists on the solid wall of his chest. But as her hands thudded against the soft silk of his shirt she knew in her heart that it wasn't him she was hitting out at but Lorraine, who had lived her life in her own self-centered way, knowing that, as their mother had always done for their father, Laurel would clear up the mess she left behind.

Roughly Hal caught her by the shoulders, pushing her away from him and holding her at arm's length.

'Lori, stop it,' he warned. 'Lori, I said stop it! You're hysterical——'

One hand left her shoulder so swiftly that she never saw it move, and she gave a small cry of pain as Hal's palm struck her cheek.

'You hit me!'

It was a cry of reproach, but even as the words left her lips she realised how carefully the slap had been planned so that it was just enough to shock her into stillness without really hurting her.

Hal smiled grimly.

'There are two traditional ways of dealing with an hysterical woman—— You surely didn't want me to kiss you?'

Laurel found that she was trembling all over, but her mind was strangely calm. Hal's action had had the desired effect and her thoughts were suddenly very clear and controlled. For the first time that evening she knew exactly what to say because, now, there was only one thing to say.

'Oh, but I do,' she breathed softly.

Hal's head went back as if she had struck him. 'You——' he began, then stopped, seeming to be having difficulty finding the words he wanted.

'I want you to kiss me, Hal. I want it more than I've ever wanted anything in my whole life.'

'But—Lori——'

It was very strange, Laurel thought with a tinge of sadness, to see this man who could use words so brilliantly in his novels now suddenly at a loss for them. Hal's bewilderment made him seem so very vulnerable, almost defenceless, no longer the cold, distant man she had at first believed him to be. Lorraine had hurt him so badly and she desperately wanted to do something to ease that hurt.

So in the end it was Laurel who took the initiative, moving towards Hal and slipping her arms around his neck, drawing his face down towards hers. At first he resisted, every muscle in his body taut, but just as she thought he was going to reject her approach completely the tension slackened and his mouth crushed hers with a fierce pressure that brought a wave of panic even as she welcomed it. But the fear vanished as swiftly as it had come and she kissed him back with all the intensity of the love and longing she had held in check for so long.

Still with her lips against Hal's, Laurel slid her hands down from his neck and over his shoulders, tracing gentle patterns across his back and down to his narrow waist. Hal's soft murmur of pleasure and the tightening of his arms around her encouraged her to further caresses as she moved her hands round to the front of his shirt, tugging impatiently at his buttons, longing to feel the warm silk of his skin under her fingers without the restriction of clothing. She felt Hal tense again, his muscles becoming taut under her wandering hands.

'Dear God, Lori,' he protested harshly. 'Don't do this to me—I won't be able to stop myself.'

'And what about me?' Laurel's voice shook, but she met his eyes confidently, letting her need show in her face without fear or hesitation. 'What if I don't want to stop you?'

A deep, contented sigh was Hal's only response, and the next moment he had swung her off her feet and carried her over to the bed, lowering her gently on to it, his hands moving to slide the one remaining strap of her dress down from her shoulder even as he released her.

The touch of his hands on her breasts was such an exquisite pleasure that Laurel felt she almost stopped breathing for a moment, and she reached up blindly to draw him down to her, revelling in the hard, warm weight of his body, her hands tangling in the soft darkness of his hair. Her need of him was every bit as strong as his desire for her, filling every inch of her body with an aching yearning that could only be appeased by the full knowledge of Hal's lovemaking, but Laurel knew that there was still one thing that had to be said before she could give herself to him completely. There could be no more deceit; *this* could not be a lie.

'Hal, wait.'

Gently she stilled his caressing hands, her own sense of loss painfully acute as he ceased the small, erotic patterns he had been tracing on her skin.

'I can't wait.' His voice was rough, hoarsely urgent. 'Lori, I *want* this!'

'I want it too,' Laurel whispered. 'Every bit as much as you—— But, Hal, you have to listen——'

Her heart clenched in distress as Hal's face darkened dangerously.

'If this is another——'

'No!' She silenced his angry words with her lips, kissing his mouth, his face, the strong column of his neck. 'No more pretence, I promise.'

His hands were rousing her again. Her dress had gone, slipping unheeded to the floor, and as his fingers moved lower, threatening to obliterate rational thought, Laurel had to struggle to retain enough control to speak.

'Please listen,' she gasped. 'I'm *not Lorraine*. I'm not your wife—I——'

'I don't give a damn who you are!' Hal broke in violently. 'I want you—*you*—whoever you are!'

Then his lips were on her breast and instinctively her body arched against his, a small, contented cry escaping her at the thought that at last she was free to love him as herself, as Laurel, with no thought of Lorraine.

Hal's touch was not gentle, but Laurel welcomed his rough caresses as evidence of his passion, her whole body coming alive under his hands so that even the brief moment of pain as she felt the powerful thrust of his body into hers, though it made her cry out, her eyes opening wide in shock, was soon forgotten in the ecstasy that followed as every thought was driven from her mind and she clung to Hal in total fulfilment.

Whether she actually slept or simply floated dreamily in a world of perfect happiness, Laurel did not know, but slowly, very slowly, she surfaced from her languorous state to the disturbing realisation that Hal was no longer beside her. Bewildered and suddenly cold with fear, she sat up, sleep blurring her eyes, and a faint sound of movement alerted her to the fact that he was still in the room.

Hal was sitting on the end of the bed, watching her. He was fully dressed, his whole body held tensely alert, like that of a predator watching its intended prey, and his face was a stony, enigmatic mask, half hidden in shadow in the faint light of early dawn. He regarded her silently for a long, taut moment, his sea-coloured eyes as dark and unfathomable as deep rock pools.

'All right,' he said at last, his voice as cold and unemotional as his face. 'I reckon you've got some explaining to do. Who the hell are you? Because one thing's for sure, you're certainly not my wife.'

CHAPTER ELEVEN

LAUREL stared at the clock in confusion and disbelief. Two o'clock! It couldn't be! But the sun streaming through the bedroom window confirmed the fact that it was indeed early afternoon. She must have slept for hours, collapsing in total exhaustion after Hal had left her.

She shuddered as she recalled the scene earlier that day, the bleakness of Hal's eyes, the immobility of his expression as he had listened to her stumbling explanation, not saying a word until she had finished, faltering to a halt, her courage dying under the unrelenting intensity of his scrutiny. The silence that descended when she stopped speaking seemed to last for ever, stretching on and on until at last Hal got slowly to his feet and moved away to stare fixedly out of the window at the horizon where the light of a new, fresh dawn was slowly breaking.

'And you expect me to believe all this?' he said flatly, keeping his face turned away from her.

'But it's the *truth*!' Laurel protested unevenly—then shrank back as Hal swung round suddenly, his eyes glittering with a cold anger.

'Is it?' he demanded harshly. 'Is it the truth or just another lie—like the one you've been living out with me?'

'It *is* the truth! Please believe me!'

'Why should I believe you?' Hal's question was a savage snarl. 'Why should this be the time you're telling the truth? I've had enough of your—Lori's—lies to last a lifetime. I wonder if even you know it all! Well, I've

167

listened to you, now it's your turn to hear what *I've* got to say—and I'll tell you all about your sister—the *truth*—if you're prepared to listen.'

Silently Laurel nodded, nerving herself for what was coming. She had to listen, and she knew it wouldn't be easy to hear the things Hal would tell her. She had learned enough of the truth about Lorraine to accept that. But Hal had the right to speak, it was time everything was out in the open at last.

'I first met Lorraine at a party at my sister's house. Max had invited her, telling Teresa he'd met her through work, that she was going through a bad patch, and he'd wanted to cheer her up. What neither Tess nor I knew was that he and Lori were already having an affair—the truth was that they'd met at a nightclub some weeks before. I should have guessed, Max has always had a roving eye and she was just his type—dressed to kill and wearing enough jewellery to sink a battleship. She looked as if she had plenty of money of her own, but what none of us knew—particularly not Max—was that none of it was paid for—it was all on credit.'

Hal pushed his hand through his dark hair, frowning at his memories.

'I thought she was a stunning woman but brittle, shallow—I didn't like her—and after the party I forgot about her until Teresa came to me in despair. She'd found out about Max and Lorraine and, to make matters worse, she'd just discovered that she was pregnant again. She begged me to help. Max works for his father's firm and he was due to be posted to their offices in Sydney in six months' time. If Tess could just hold their marriage together until then, Max would be thousands of miles away from Lorraine and she was sure they'd be able to start again.'

Hal was suddenly silent, absorbed in his own thoughts, and Laurel waited quietly, sensing intuitively that it was best to leave him to tell the story in his own way. Knowing his deep love for his family, a love that had come out so strongly in his novel, she could well imagine how much his sister's appeal for help had meant to him. Drawing a deep breath, Hal began again.

'I decided to contact Lorraine. If she could be persuaded to stop seeing Max, their affair would die a natural death—and I had a strong card to use against her. I'd found out about her financial situation. She had a brief spell as a model, but suddenly her face wasn't popular any more and she couldn't get work. She'd run up massive debts, she was months behind with the rent on her flat, but she'd had a taste of the good life and she couldn't adjust to being without it. She still wanted the clothes, the nightclubs, a car—everything.'

He had been prowling restlessly around the room as he spoke, but now he came to a halt, his eyes fixed on Laurel's pale face.

'She was up to her neck in debt and she didn't deny it. But she wasn't keen to let Max go—said she'd always wanted a wealthy husband who could keep her in luxury—so I pointed out a few home truths, like the fact that even if Max did divorce Teresa there would be alimony to pay—three children to support. I told her that if she really wanted to marry a wealthy man she'd be better off marrying me.'

'*What!*'

Laurel's head came up sharply. Ever since Hal had begun his story she had been fighting for control, waiting for the moment she dreaded, the moment when Hal would tell her that he'd got to know Lorraine better, changed his mind about her—fallen in love with her, so to hear his account of his marriage proposal stated in such stark, emotionless terms came as such a shock that she couldn't believe what she had heard.

'You——'

'I offered Lorraine marriage if she'd leave Max alone and give Teresa a chance to make things work. It was to be a marriage in name only—purely a business deal—though, of course, Max wasn't to know that. It was only to last the six months until he and Teresa were on their way to Australia. It had to be marriage, though, because by then it had become obvious that nothing less would put my brother-in-law——' Hal grimaced as if the words tasted sour in his mouth '—off seeing her. In return I'd clear her debts, give her a generous allowance while she was living with me, and when the six months were up I'd arrange for a divorce and provide the sort of financial settlement that would give her the life she wanted.'

'And—she agreed?' Laurel's voice came and went unevenly. She was still having trouble adjusting to the fact that her sister's marriage to Hal had been a purely material one, with nothing emotional about it, not even a hint of the desire Hal had shown towards herself.

In her mind, phrases heard and not fully understood surfaced like bubbles floating to the top of a glass. The conditions that would be 'no more difficult than before'; 'You agreed to act as my wife *again*'; and, infinitely more disturbing because she didn't dare to try to interpret it, 'It's different this time...'

'She didn't say yes immediately. I gave her time to think, but it didn't take long. The very next day she appeared on my doorstep, ready to agree to everything I'd offered, and so——' Hal spread his hands in a gesture of resignation '—we were married. I paid all her debts as I'd promised—those she'd acquired before the marriage and plenty that came after it. She had a spending spree as soon as she was legally my wife—bought herself a car, for one thing.'

Laurel nodded silently, remembering the sleek white sports car Lorraine had been driving, the car she had crashed, killing herself and injuring Jenny and so forcing Laurel to seek out Hal in the first place.

'I kept my side of the bargain and she kept hers—for four months. Then one morning she just disappeared.'

'But why?'

His smile was bleak. 'She left me a note. In it she told me quite bluntly that she'd thought she could keep to the terms of our agreement, but now she realised that she'd made a mistake. She said—and I quote—that she'd thought one rich man was as good as another but she'd been wrong, so she couldn't keep to the six months we'd agreed on. But there were only two months left——'

Only two months left. Now Laurel knew why Hal had imposed those conditions at their first meeting, why he had stipulated that particular length of time. He had intended to keep Lorraine to the letter of their agreement—but it hadn't been Lorraine who had had to fulfil those conditions but her twin—Laurel herself.

'She went back to Max,' she said shakily, remembering the letter about the hotel booking she had found among Lorraine's clothes.

'Yes.' The single syllable was as cold and hard as Hal's eyes. 'I tried to find her, but she'd vanished without a trace.'

But Max had never turned up at the meeting Lorraine had arranged—he'd admitted so himself. So what had gone wrong?

'I didn't know about this——'

'No,' Hal sighed wearily, 'I don't suppose you did. You'd never have come here if you had—unless—' the blue eyes narrowed speculatively, 'unless this whole story is another pack of lies hatched up between the two of you to——'

'No!' Laurel cried desperately, shaking her head violently. 'Lorraine's dead! Whatever she did, she's paid for it! She's *dead*!'

She choked on the last word, tears spilling out over her cheeks and she bent her head, hiding her face in her hands. She heard Hal move swiftly and come to her side. His touch on her shoulder was very gentle.

'I'm sorry,' he said huskily. 'That was cruel of me. But I had to be sure—you can see that, can't you?'

Laurel could only nod in response. Lorraine had used Hal, had behaved with total carelessness for his sister's feelings; she couldn't blame him for his cynical suspicions.

'Lorraine is——' she began brokenly, but Hal laid two fingers over her mouth to silence her.

'I know,' he said sombrely. 'The problem now is what we do about you.'

She raised shocked, tear-bright eyes to his face.

'You don't have to do anything about me!'

'Oh, but I do. I feel I owe you something, especially after what's happened.'

'Oh, no!' Laurel's voice shook in dismay. She couldn't bear it if he felt obliged to make it up to her—if he felt ashamed of having made love to her. 'Forget about that!' she blurted out unthinkingly. 'It was nothing!'

'*Nothing!*' he echoed incredulously. 'But you were a virgin and I——'

Laurel had thought she was beyond feeling any more pain, but now she knew that she had still one more performance to give, beside which the part she had been playing would be nothing at all. Lorraine had taken everything Hal offered and then walked out, *she* couldn't take any more. And what made it so very much worse was the fact that Hal was only offering help because he felt obliged to after he had made love to her—an act which he now clearly deeply regretted.

'It had to happen some time,' she said, assuming a tone of brittle carelessness that was very far from what she was really feeling. 'After all, I am twenty-two. Virginity's thoroughly unfashionable nowadays, didn't you know?'

The knowledge that she had succeeded far better than she had hoped tore Laurel's heart in two as she saw Hal visibly withdraw from her, the concerned expression fading from his eyes, leaving them hard as stone.

'I see,' he said slowly, scathingly. 'How very liberated of you to take it that way!'

She forced herself to smile, though her lips felt stiff and wooden.

'We're both adults. It was what we both wanted at the time. There's no need for anyone to feel guilty about it.' She couldn't meet Hal's eyes, afraid of what she might see there, but she heard him draw in his breath sharply with a sound like the hiss of an angry snake.

'You're Lorraine's sister all right,' he declared harshly. 'I've never met two women who were more alike!'

Then he turned on his heel and was gone, leaving Laurel with her heart so devastated that she could not even find release in tears, because the thing she had most dreaded had happened. Hal had said that she was very like Lorraine because she had been unable to let him see the one vital difference between herself and her twin— the fact that she loved him more than life itself.

Wearily she came back to the present, her eyes going to the copy of *Chase the Dawn* that lay on the bedside table. With a sigh she picked it up, staring blankly at the cover. 'Even on the darkest night of your life, you can always chase the dawn.' A laugh, as bitter as any of Hal's, rose in her throat as she remembered how, only the day before, she had believed that she had lived through the darkest night of her life. Beside the anguish she felt now, that pain seemed like the merest pinprick.

Would things have been any different if she and Hal *had* met as the complete strangers they had tried to pretend to be, if Hal had never been Lorraine's husband?

Laurel knew she was deluding herself to think so. Even when he had revealed the passion he had felt—and fought against—Hal had spoken only of his desire, there had been no words of love. And last night—tears burned in her eyes at the memory—last night both of them had been caught up in a whirlwind. Hal had wanted her desperately, the fierce, raging passion inside him too strong to be contained any longer. But desire was all he had felt and already he deeply regretted having made love to her. She had never really touched his heart, and cold realism told her that even if he had met her first instead of Lorraine, nothing would have changed.

There was only one thing she could do, and that was to pack her bags and go, get out of Hal's life for ever. No, there was one other thing she must do; she could never live with herself if she didn't.

Getting out of bed, Laurel dressed swiftly in a simple blouse and skirt, her own clothes, taken from the few she had brought with her. She had no right to the ones Hal had bought. Then she picked up her handbag and took out her cheque book. Her heart ached as she thought of Jenny and she prayed that somehow she could make her little sister understand what she was doing. Ruthlessly she forced such thoughts away; she couldn't allow anything to make her weaken now.

Even to write Hal's name hurt so much that her hand shook and hot tears blurred her vision. *Stop it!* she told herself fiercely. There would be time enough for tears later; she would have the rest of her life in which to weep. Now she had to be strong. With the cheque in her hand she made her way downstairs.

The murmur of voices reached her from behind the closed door of the living-room. She could hear Jan's light tones distinctly. Please, she prayed, let Hal be with her so that I don't have to face him again!

Moving softly, she crossed the hall and opened the door to Hal's study—then froze, every trace of colour leaving her cheeks as Hal, who was seated at his desk, lifted his head in response to the sound of the door opening. For a long moment blue eyes locked with green, Laurel's heart beating rapidly high up in her throat. Hal's face was haggard, lines of strain etched around his nose and mouth, and his eyes were bleak, empty of all emotion. Suddenly he seemed to recollect himself and got to his feet.

'Was there something you wanted?' he asked, his tone far from encouraging.

Somehow Laurel found the strength to move into the room, pushing the door closed behind her.

'Yes, I—I wanted to give you this.'

She held out the cheque which she had made out for the full amount of the money Hal had given her. Hal stared at it blankly as if he didn't recognise it for what it was, then at last he shook his head slowly.

'No, Lori—Laurel——' He amended the name with difficulty. 'Keep the money. If I can't give you anything else, at least I can give you that.'

Bitter agony seared through her. He was still trying to make amends for having made love to her.

'I want you to have it back,' she declared in a voice that was high and tight with the effort of hiding her distress from him as she thrust the piece of paper at him. Hal scowled savagely.

'Don't you think you've earned it?' he snarled.

'No!' Laurel choked on the word. 'Not like this! I can't take your money when I lied to get it!'

Hal was suddenly very still, a deep frown darkening his face, then, slowly, he held out his hand. Without hesitation she put the cheque into it, then stared in blank amazement as, never taking his eyes from her face, he tore the paper to shreds, scattering the tiny pieces on the carpet in front of him.

'Why did you do that?'

'Because I don't want the money back,' he told her flatly. 'Do you think I'd let a child of Jenny's age suffer if there was anything I could do to prevent it?'

So she had been right. A devastating mixture of delight and despair assailed her at the thought that her instincts had been correct, that Hal was too caring a person to have refused to help—if only she had had the courage to tell him the truth from the start.

'It's only money,' Hal added cynically. 'And money's one thing I've got plenty of.'

'I'll pay it all back,' she told him earnestly. 'Every penny. I'll——'

'Will you shut up about the bloody money!' he exploded. 'I am giving it to you.' He used his hands to emphasise the words. 'Let that be an end of it!'

'But——' she tried again, but her voice failed her as Hal's head came up suddenly. The look he gave her had such a terrible, suppressed violence in it that instinctively she took a hasty step backwards, blundering into a small table on which lay a thick pile of neatly typed manuscript, sending the papers cascading to the floor.

'Oh, I'm sorry!' This had to be the manuscript of the book Hal had been working on, his new novel. Hot colour washing her cheeks, Laurel crouched down to pick up the fallen papers.

With a violent curse Hal lunged forward, his fingers closing over her wrist. But she had already retrieved some of the pages and now she stared blankly at one of them, unable to believe what she saw.

The page she held bore only a single line—a dedication—the typed inscription reading simply 'For Lori'. But the name Lori had been crossed out—and very recently too, because the ink had smudged slightly in the fall from the table. Above the original dedication the words 'For Laurel' had been written in strong black letters.

She turned a bewildered face to Hal, trying to read the emotion that darkened his eyes.

'I don't understand,' she said slowly. 'What does this mean?'

His mouth twisted bitterly as he released her wrist and straightened up, rubbing a hand across his eyes in a gesture of weariness and defeat.

'It means,' he said harshly, 'that I was fool enough to want to dedicate my book to the woman I love—and I'm still fool enough to want to do it even when I find she's not actually the woman I thought she was.'

Very slowly Laurel got to her feet, her legs feeling like cotton wool beneath her.

'Who—is the woman you love?' she asked jerkily.

Hal's smile was slow and sardonic.

'Can't you guess, Laurel?' he asked with gentle mockery. 'Is it so very hard?'

Her throat was suddenly painfully dry and she had to swallow hard several times before she could speak.

'I daren't guess,' she said unsteadily. 'I'm afraid I might be wrong.'

'Afraid?' His question came very softly. 'Why should you be afraid?'

He was watching her intently now, his blue eyes wary but with a flicker of some other, stronger emotion showing in their depths. Laurel met his searching gaze bravely.

'Wouldn't any woman be afraid if she thought the thing she wanted most in the world might just be within her grasp but she didn't know if she dared reach out and take it?' she said, knowing she was taking a terrible gamble. If she had misunderstood what Hal was saying, she was laying herself open to the most devastating destruction of the tiny, fragile flame of hope that had lit up inside her.

He closed his eyes briefly and when he opened them again she saw they were as dark and deep as the sea at midnight.

'Laurel,' he said slowly, hoarsely, 'if you're saying what I think you're saying, for God's sake tell me plainly. You——?'

'I love you, Hal,' she broke in swiftly, unable to bear the raw emotion in his voice. 'I love you with all my heart. There,' she added, her voice lifting because the sudden flare of delight in his eyes told her she had not misunderstood him, 'is that plain enough?'

'You can't.' Hal's voice was husky. 'You can't fall in love with someone you've only known for a week.'

'Why not? Your grandmother did,' she reminded him gently. Her spirits leapt at Hal's swift smile.

'So she did,' he admitted. 'And so did I.'

A long sigh escaped Laurel. 'With me?' she asked, needing desperately to be sure, to hear him say it. Hal's sudden laugh, a warm, genuine sound, not the bitter one she so hated, made her heart soar.

'Who else?' he demanded. 'There were times this week when I didn't know what the hell was happening to me, but the one thing I was sure of was the fact that you're the most beautiful, most desirable creature I've ever set eyes on. But there's more to it than that. I don't just desire you—I love everything about you—and I need you. I need you to be with me every day, wherever I am, whatever I do. I—I love you, Laurel,' he finished simply.

'Oh, Hal!' It was a cry of joy and Laurel would have flung herself into his arms, but the sudden sobering of his expression stilled the movement as her heart twisted in apprehension. 'It's Lorraine, isn't it?' she whispered. Even now, her sister still cast a shadow over them.

'Yes, Lorraine,' Hal said slowly. 'I've done a lot of thinking about my time with your sister, and I have to admit that I'm not very proud of what I've found out about myself.'

As Laurel opened her mouth to protest he shook his head to silence her.

'I never knew Lorraine, Laurel, not really. We never knew each other. She saw only what she wanted to see— my money, my position—but I only ever knew the part of her she let me see, the woman she was pretending to be. She never told me anything about her life before I met her—your father, the financial problems. She even pretended that you and Jenny didn't exist. And I didn't try to get to know her better. Once she had my ring on her finger and my money in her bank account I thought that was all she needed, and I ignored her and concentrated on my work.'

Lorraine's voice, harsh and bitter with accusations of Hal's neglect, rang in Laurel's ears—and there was something else, something the stresses of the previous night had driven from her mind until now.

'I was working on a new novel—that novel.' He gestured towards the pile of manuscript. 'And—' the glance he shot at Laurel was shamefaced, filled with wry, self-mocking humour, 'well, you've seen what I can be like when I'm writing.'

'But you made time to be with me,' Laurel said quietly, and he nodded silent agreement, his expression thoughtful.

'That was when I knew something was happening that I didn't really understand. Nothing has ever come between me and my work before. When I'm writing, the world could cease to exist and I wouldn't notice—but I couldn't forget about *you*. I tried to cut you out of my mind, tried to concentrate on what I was doing, but you always came creeping back into my thoughts until I found

I was resenting the time I spent working because it took up time I could be spending with you. That never happened with Lorraine.'

Hal's eyes, which had been so clear and bright, were now clouded and touched with a shadow of regret.

'Perhaps if I'd taken some time to talk to her—if I'd found out about your father, your childhood—I'd have seen how those events had made her the person she was. Maybe I could even have helped her. But all I saw was a predatory, grasping woman who threatened my sister's happiness. Max may be all kinds of a louse, but Tess loves him and he's the father of her children.'

A savage anger darkened Hal's face at the thought of his brother-in-law.

'I doubt if Lorraine got much joy from that relationship,' he said sombrely. 'He let drop a few truths about what happened last night. I was too angry to take them in then, but I've had time to think about them since. For one thing—on the day I offered Lorraine marriage she saw Max that same evening. Apparently she came clean about her financial situation and once he knew the facts he backed out pretty fast. Max wouldn't look at a woman who didn't have money of her own. His father is a very wealthy man, but he keeps a pretty tight grip on the purse-strings. Max has his salary, nothing more, and when you live life at the pace he does you need plenty of cash. He thought Lorraine was rich—she certainly gave that impression—but when he found out she wasn't he didn't want to know her. It must have been as a result of his desertion that she accepted my offer. Perhaps she thought the money I could give her would be enough, in spite of the lack of any emotional involvement, or perhaps she believed that when Max saw her with someone else he'd come running back. I don't know. Either way, it didn't work. Then, when she left me, she contacted Max again. She made arrangements to meet him.'

Laurel nodded. 'There was a letter in her suitcase—a hotel booking—but Max never turned up.'

'No.' Hal's tone was grim. 'By that time he'd learned what side his bread was buttered. Archie Kennington— Max's father—is a very conventional man. He'd heard rumours of the Lorraine affair and turned on the heavy father act. If Max had continued to see Lorraine he was likely to find himself cut off without the proverbial penny, and that wasn't a risk he was prepared to take.'

'But he still made a play for me, believing me to be Lorraine.'

'I know. I'm afraid my brother-in-law's a greedy man. He always wants what he can't have. But perhaps this new start in Australia will work things out. That and the fright he got last night—I think he really believed I might actually kill him. I hope so, for Teresa's sake. I'm only sorry that she—and Lorraine—got involved with someone like him in the first place. The truth is, he's incapable of loving anyone except himself.'

In her head Laurel could hear her twin's voice. 'I married the wrong man, Lauri. Hal seemed to have everything I was looking for and he didn't have a wife, so...' She had taken that 'wrong man' simply to mean that Hal wasn't right for Lorraine, but now she realised that her sister had meant that Hal was the wrong man because he wasn't Max. He was as wealthy as Max appeared to be and, unlike Max, he had not been married. Laurel thought she could understand how, starved of the luxury that was so important to her, Lorraine might have seen Hal's proposal as the answer to everything. By marrying Hal she would have her revenge on the man who had rejected her and at the same time acquire a husband who could give her the lifestyle she craved. But she had reckoned without her own feelings.

Because now, at last, Laurel saw that she had been completely wrong in believing that every time Lorraine spoke she had been talking about Hal. Somewhere in that muttered comment she hadn't been able to catch her twin must have mentioned Max's name, and it had been *Max* she had meant when she had said, 'I loved him, Lauri, I really loved him—but he just used me. He didn't care how I felt, all he thought about was money—money—*money*!'

'I think she really cared about Max,' she said quietly, and Hal nodded agreement, his expression sombre.

'I believe she did and, after all you've told me about your father, I can understand that when he rejected her she really believed that money could buy her happiness. It was her appalling bad luck to give her heart to an amoral bastard like Max, someone who could beat her at her own game.'

His eyes went to Laurel's face and she saw the sincere regret that burned in them.

'I know it's too late, for Lorraine, but I'm truly sorry that I didn't take the trouble to get to know her, to find out what was behind her behaviour.'

Laurel's smile was touched with sadness, but her eyes shone with a reflection of the glow that had lit up in her heart. She knew how hard Hal had found it to admit his mistakes, but he had done it openly and unreservedly, and by doing so he had given her back something of the sister she had loved. Lorraine had had her faults, she had used Hal and Teresa for her own selfish ends, but she was still her twin, almost a part of her, and she couldn't have borne to lose her completely. Now, because of Hal's generous honesty, she knew that at last she could live at peace with her memories of Lorraine.

'I'm afraid that Lorraine was very much my father's daughter. They both believed that money was the answer to everything.'

'But you don't,' Hal put in quickly. 'That's what bothered me from the beginning. You started out in true Lorraine style, asking for money, apparently prepared to do anything to get it, but then you were so scrupulously honest about other things. You fought like hell when I bought you clothes, you tried to find things to do to *earn* the money I'd given you, tried to give me back some money that wasn't part of our bargain—you even asked my permission to use the phone! Lori would never have thought to do that, she'd just have gone ahead and used it. I couldn't believe what was happening. I was convinced you were Lorraine, and yet you behaved in ways she never would. You coped with Jet's paw, you were quite content with the simple things like exploring the Brigg. You didn't ask for the luxuries I expected to have to provide. You even cared about my work, made sure I had the time to do it, talked to me about it. I didn't know what to think. I didn't believe that Lori could have changed so much. Only you weren't Lori, and that made all the difference.'

'I did try to tell you,' Laurel reminded him softly.

'I know,' he said ruefully, 'and I was too bloody-minded to listen. But I had no reason to believe you could be anyone else. Lori had been so adamant that she had no family, and it was typical of her to come looking for me when she needed money. Then, to complicate matters even further, I found that I couldn't keep my distance as I'd always done before. I was stunned to find that I wanted to kiss you, and when I did I forgot about everything else. All I knew was that I had to get that glorious body of yours into my bed under any circumstances, that I'd do anything to get you there. And that was something I'd never felt about Lorraine.'

'You said she was a stunning woman. Didn't you ever desire her too?'

'No!' The answer came sharply and with such a ring of conviction that there was no need for Hal to say any more, but he continued swiftly, 'Lorraine was a beautiful woman—how could I say otherwise when she looked so like you?—but she left me cold. There was a brittleness about her, a shallowness that destroyed the impact of her looks. To be honest, the first time I saw you you looked so tired and drawn that you were only a shadow of the woman I'd known—and yet I wanted to kiss you. I never even kissed your sister, but suddenly it was the thing I wanted most in all the world. I was furious with myself, furious that I could feel that way about someone I didn't even like. But as soon as my lips touched yours everything changed. I wanted that kiss and I wanted more, much more. I'd been quite convinced that all I wanted to do was to make Lori fulfil our agreement. There were only a few weeks to go before Max and Tess left for Sydney, and if I could keep her here, away from London, then their marriage might still have a chance. I didn't know what had happened between Lori and Max, all I thought was that she was here and that she'd given me the weapon to use against her on a plate. I thought it would be just as it had been before—a marriage in name only—and I'd had no trouble keeping to that with Lorraine. But I couldn't keep to it with you.'

Once more Hal pushed a hand through the dark sleekness of his hair, the gesture mirroring the disturbed state of his thoughts.

'That's when I thought I was going crazy, especially when I found that I couldn't just use you for two months and then discard you because you were so very different from what I expected—and I found I liked what you were.'

At last he reached out and touched Laurel's cheek very gently as if to reassure himself that she was real.

'I found that even though I wanted you so much that just to be in the same room as you and not touch you was hell on earth, I couldn't just take you for my own pleasure alone. I could have done that the night I put you to bed—you were too tired to resist me—but I wanted *you* to feel something too, especially after you told me about your father and made me see the past in a very different light. I understood then how insecure you—and Lori—must have felt, and I wanted to help. I think that was when I realised that I was truly in love with you, so I went to London and told the Lorrimers not to come here—I didn't want anything to interfere with the relationship I believed we were starting to build. I couldn't wait to get back to you. But when I arrived and you were out I thought you'd gone to see Max, and I almost went out of my head.'

'I'd gone to see Jenny. I had to—I didn't know how I could go through with things if it wasn't for her,' Laurel put in quietly, and Hal sighed.

'I know that now, but at the time all I could think of was the way I felt about you and the sheer, blind jealousy that filled me at the thought of you with Max. That's why I didn't stop him from coming here. I had to see you and him together. I had to know how you felt about him—— But, of course, it was Lori I was trying to test, not you. I think, deep in my heart, I really knew you were someone else—Lori could never have changed so much in such a short time.'

'Poor Lori,' sighed Laurel, her heart filling with pity for her twin who had made such a mess of her life.

'Poor Lori,' Hal agreed soberly, drawing her gently towards him. 'But at least one good thing came out of all that. If it hadn't been for Lorraine I'd never have met you. I only wish I'd seen you first, or met you both at the same time. Even though you are so amazingly alike, I'm damn sure I'd have known you were the one for me.'

His arms came round her gently, almost hesitantly.

'When I think of how I treated you when you were already going through hell!' he groaned in self-reproach. 'Can you ever forgive me?'

'If you'll forgive me for the way I deceived you,' Laurel answered, letting herself relax against him and lifting her face for his kiss.

'Forgiven and forgotten,' Hal murmured against her lips, then his arms tightened round her possessively and as Laurel responded eagerly to his kiss she knew that there was no need to talk any more of forgiveness of the past, only the bright dawn and the golden future that lay ahead of them.

The sound of a door opening and a voice calling Hal's name brought them back to the real world at last. Still cradling Laurel against him, he smiled ruefully.

'I'd forgotten you have a visitor—a Mrs Howard.'

'Barbara! What's Barbara doing here? Oh, my God!' The glowing colour fled from Laurel's cheeks. 'Jenny!'

'Calm down, love,' soothed Hal. 'Jenny's fine, and you don't have to care for her on your own any more. I can help you—we'll do it together. Barbara rang here early this morning to let you know that the doctors think Jenny will be fit to travel much sooner than they expected—next week, in fact. I asked her to come here because I thought you'd need someone to take you home. I felt sure you'd leave after what had happened, and I couldn't bear the thought of you being alone and unhappy.'

Laurel lifted a hand to touch his cheek gently, feeling she could lose herself in the dark, loving depths of his eyes.

'I'll never be alone—or unhappy—again, not now I've found you.'

In the hall Jan called Hal's name a second time, and he sighed.

'We'll have to join them,' he said reluctantly. 'This is going to take some explaining. We'll have to tell Jan that the woman she thought I was married to isn't really my wife but——'

His voice changed suddenly, deepening and growing husky as he took Laurel's hand in his.

'But she will be, just as soon as it can be arranged.' Blue eyes looked deep into Laurel's green ones, searching for the answer he needed. 'That *is* how it's going to be, isn't it?'

Laurel's smile was radiant.

'Oh, yes, my love, that's exactly how it's going to be.'

Harlequin Presents

Coming Next Month

1199   THE ALOHA BRIDE   Emma Darcy
Robyn is at a low point in her life and is determined not to be hurt again. Then she meets Julian Lassiter. Somehow she finds herself wanting to solve Julian's problems in a way that is not only reckless but is positively dangerous!

1200   FANTASY LOVER   Sally Heywood
Torrin Anthony's arrival in Merril's life is unwanted and upsetting, for this shallow, artificial actor reminds her of Azur—the heroic rebel sympathizer who'd rescued her from cross fire in the Middle East. Could she possibly be mixing fantasy with reality?

1201   WITHOUT TRUST   Penny Jordan
Lark Cummings, on trial for crimes she's innocent of, hasn't a chance when she is faced with James Wolfe's relentless prosecution. Then the case is inexplicably dropped. She wants to hate this formidable man, but finds it impossible when fate brings him back into her life!

1202   DESPERATION   Charlotte Lamb
Megan accepts a year apart from her newfound love, Devlin Hurst—she'll wait for him. Yet when her life turns upside down just hours after his departure, she knows she must break their pact. Only she has to lie to do it.

1203   TAKE AWAY THE PRIDE   Emma Richmond
Toby lies about her qualifications to become secretary to powerful Marcus du Mann—and is a disaster. But when Marcus gets stuck with his baby nephew, Toby is put in charge. And she's coping well—until Marcus decides to move in and help....

1204   TOKYO TRYST   Kay Thorpe
Two years ago, Alex walked out on Greg Wilde when she discovered he was unfaithful. Now they're on the same work assignment in Japan. Despite Greg's obvious interest in the beautiful Yuki, Alex finds herself falling in love with him all over again!

1205   IMPULSIVE GAMBLE   Lynn Turner
Free-lance journalist Abbie desperately wants a story on reclusive engineer-inventor Malacchi Garrett. Then she discovers the only way to get close to him is by living a lie. But how can she lie to the man she's falling in love with?

1206   NO GENTLE LOVING   Sara Wood
Hostile suspicion from wealthy Dimitri Kastelli meets Helen in Crete, where she's come to find out about the mother she never knew. What grudge could he hold against a long-dead peasant woman? And how would he react if he learned who Helen is?

Available in September wherever paperback books are sold, or through Harlequin Reader Service:

In the U.S.
901 Fuhrmann Blvd.
P.O. Box 1397
Buffalo, N.Y. 14240-1397

In Canada
P.O. Box 603
Fort Erie, Ontario
L2A 5X3

The sun, the surf, the sand...

One relaxing month by the sea was all Zoe,
Diana and Gracie ever expected from their
four-week stay at Gull Cottage, the luxurious
East Hampton mansion. They never thought
that what they found at the beach would
change their lives forever.

Join Zoe, Diana and Gracie for the summer of
their lives. Don't miss the GULL COTTAGE
trilogy in Harlequin American Romance: #301
CHARMED CIRCLE by Robin Francis (July
1989); #305 MOTHER KNOWS BEST by
Barbara Bretton (August 1989); and #309
SAVING GRACE by Anne McAllister
(September 1989).

GULL COTTAGE—because one month can be
the start of forever...

You'll flip . . . your pages won't!
Read paperbacks *hands-free* with

Book Mate • I

The perfect "mate" for all your romance paperbacks
Traveling • Vacationing • At Work • In Bed • Studying
• Cooking • Eating

Perfect size for all standard paperbacks, this wonderful invention makes reading a pure pleasure! Ingenious design holds paperback books OPEN and FLAT so even wind can't ruffle pages — leaves your hands free to do other things. Reinforced, wipe-clean vinyl-covered holder flexes to let you turn pages without undoing the strap . . . supports paperbacks so well, they have the strength of hardcovers!

Pages turn WITHOUT opening the strap

SEE-THROUGH STRAP

Reinforced back stays flat

Built in bookmark

BOOK MARK

BACK COVER
HOLDING STRIP

10 x 7¼ . opened
Snaps closed for easy carrying, too

Available now. Send your name, address, and zip code, along with a check or money order for just $5.95 + .75¢ for postage & handling (for a total of $6.70) payable to Reader Service to:

Reader Service
Bookmate Offer
901 Fuhrmann Blvd.
P.O. Box 1396
Buffalo, N.Y. 14269-1396

Offer not available in Canada
*New York and Iowa residents add appropriate sales tax.

BM-G

Harlequin Regency Romance™

Romance the way it was *always* meant to be!

The time is 1811, when a Regent Prince rules the empire. The place is London, the glittering capital where rakish dukes and dazzling debutantes scheme and flirt in a dangerously exciting game. Where marriage is the passport to wealth and power, yet every girl hopes secretly for love....

Welcome to Harlequin Regency Romance where reading is an adventure and romance is *not* just a thing of the past! Two delightful books a month.

Available wherever Harlequin Books are sold.

LOST

MOON FLOWER

TO BE FOUND...
lots of romance & adventure
in Harlequin's
3000th Romance

THE LOST MOON FLOWER
Bethany Campbell

Available wherever Harlequin Books
are sold this August.

"NEW"

Harlequin Historicals

Storytelling at its best
by some of your favorite authors such as
Kristen James, Nora Roberts, Cassie Edwards

Strong, independent heroines
Heroes you'll fall in love with
Compelling love stories

History has never been so romantic.

Look for them now wherever Harlequin Books are sold.